The OCTOBER Season

A COLLECTION OF SPOOKY TALES BY
JUNO JAKOB

CONTENTS

Introduction

INTRODUCTION

Autumn, October, Halloween.

I cannot think of three more beautiful words in the English language. The feelings they conjure are as precious to me as memories of an innocent childhood. Jack-O'-Lanterns as important as Sunday dinner with family. The smell and texture of dead fall leaves as crucial as afternoons playing with friends down at 'The Den'. Every day of October as joyous as Christmas Day. November 1st to October 1st is simply too long! But, I suppose October being just once a year just makes it more special and rare.

I wrote these stories thinking over those three wonderful words, as well as a few dozen more words I rediscovered through word association. I say rediscovered as I found memories and feelings from past Octobers I had long forgotten and thought lost forever.

I write them now so they never be forgotten again.

Juno Jakob

Hawthorne Hotel
Salem, Massachusetts

THE OCTOBER SEASON

OCTOBER

October.

October, what a wonderful word.
October, what a breathtaking time.
October, what a completely intoxicating feeling of
pure joy and excitement.

The month of October was to live in
darkness and warmth as well as in light and the cold.
Smoke rises from chimneys, puffing out like black
cotton candy as the autumn chill hung in the air.
It gave a comforting feeling you never wanted to end.
The heavy thick coats come out of cupboards
and for some, scarfs and mittens. An uncanny wind

howls through the shedding trees, trees that reach to the grey sky like skeletal hands.

The nights, the time when things really come alive, were longer. A bump in the night sends chills down the spine and goosebumps up the arms as the imagination, if it were in fact just that, runs wild with ghosts, monsters and ghouls hiding under beds and behind curtains.

The rain on the window has a different sound than it does in say, February or April. It was almost like the tapping was the voice of the shadow on the moon.

The adults go about their normal lives but ah, they know not of the season's power and spell. It's a time where you can smell the bonfires burning and the pumpkins growing. A time to see the fall colours and mist clinging low. There's the feeling, the strongest one imaginable, that anything might happen during any of the thirty nights of the month to be revealed in all its glory in the morning.

On the outskirts of town, stunning pumpkin patches are full of wonderful specimens just ready for carving into Jack-O'-Lanterns of all different faces, each more wicked and twisted than the last.

There's the ecstatic rush during the early days of the month when the seasonal aisle in the supermarket, usually reserved for Easter eggs and summer garden furniture, is decorated with black and orange or sometimes green and purple signage and all the boxes full of treats, horror masks, grotesque costumes and macabre decorations are ready to go onto the shelf for just less than thirty precious days until that oh so special final day of the month. The day you spend all year planning a costume for, the day you spend meticulously planning a face for the biggest pumpkin you can find, the day you plan out which houses to trick or treat at and which neighbour is handing out the best treats and which neighbour deserves a devilish trick. The day where, if you were lucky, you can speak directly to the spirits and hear their stories as the sun sets and grows old letting the still night come and the rituals begin.

Samhain, All Saints Day, Day Of The Dead, All Hallows Eve.

HALLOWEEN.

The most special and wondrous night of all the year, full of mischief, magic and spooky goings on.

To be alive during the very month was a privilege.

Delightful, mysterious, ghostly, frightening October.

As the last day of September 1990 slips away with the stroke of midnight and a storm comes across the skies, the sleepy little town of Port Hampton falls under October's autumn spell…

THE SCARECROW

"Have you seen it?" Cathryn King asked without looking up from the morning newspaper.

Miles took a moment to register the question his wife had asked as he poured coffee into his usual mug. "Seen what, sorry?"

"Our friend in the yard," she pointed to the window.

Miles peered out toward the corn field and saw it.

"Did you put it there?" he frowned.

Cathryn shook her head and continued to read about the October festivities in town that day.

Miles stood and admired the scarecrow pitched before him. It looked no better or no worse than any other scarecrow he had seen in the surrounding fields.

It had a wide brimmed black hat, a tatty black suit with a dirty white shirt and a western tie. Its face nothing more than odd buttons stitched to a burlap sack and a sewn up frown.

A crucified southern preacher on a cross made of large dead branches.

"Do you think it was Bruce's kids?" Miles asked.

"I'm not sure, I thought they were with their mother for the week," Cathryn replied.

"No one else around here comes to the farm..." he murmured more to himself. "Should I take it down?"

"It's Halloween. Might be a good decoration," she reasoned hopefully.

"You know I don't go for that stuff," he muttered, stepping closer to the scarecrow. "It might keep the birds away I suppose."

Cathryn spent the afternoon in town working in the Carnegie library while Miles spent the day in the field under the watchful eye of the scarecrow as he governed over his eight acres of land from the seat of his tractor.

The year had been good to him and he and Cathryn had a wonderful crop ready for harvesting. He figured they'd have enough to pay off the tractor loan and be able to put a bit of money aside for the rainy day fund they never managed to find spare money for.

The hair on his neck prickled. He kept fighting the urge to catch a glance over his shoulder. Its button eyes burned in his mind. It was just a scarecrow and nothing more, nothing but straw and an old pastor's suit...but it still stood. Watching. It had stood gazing without offering Miles a cooling drink or a helping hand.

Miles found it best not to look at it and continue his work in the mild autumn chill until the pain in his leg became too much for him.

When she returned home in the early evening, Cathryn found Miles sitting on the porch steps facing towards the suited visitor on their farm.

"Watch your step!" he warned as she walked toward him carrying a stack of books.

She stopped and her eyes followed his pointed finger to the spot near her feet.

A dead crow. Its wings spread and its talons up in the air, its beak in a silent cry.

"Oh no!" she startled, taking a side step.

"Watch your step I said!" Miles called again before she planted her right foot back on the ground.

Her foot nearly crushed another dead crow.

It was then that Cathryn saw the ground between the porch steps and the start of the crops was littered with dead birds.

Crows, Magpies, Robins and Wood pigeons.

"There's fifteen," Miles counted.

"Oh dear…What…" she began baffled. "Do you think there's bad bird food somewhere…or cats?"

"Maybe. They don't seem broken at all," he shrugged.

"So sad," Cathryn observed, carefully sitting down beside her husband. "So many at once.…"

"I could bury 'em somewhere," Miles thought out loud.

"I don't like the idea of that," Cathryn disagreed quietly. "Seems such a shame."

"I know…maybe Mr. Lutz would take them for his taxidermy collection."

"Make something beautiful from death," Cathryn mused.

Miles got a cardboard box from under the stairs then carefully placed each bird inside it before driving them over to Mr. Lutz's house three miles down the road.

*

Cathryn stood in the yard sipping her second cup of tea since arriving home. She looked out at the crop they had grown and thought how it would help with the elusive rainy day fund they had often dreamed of… Or maybe a holiday away from Port Hampton? Somewhere warm and exciting. A young girl named Cecilie who also worked at the library had visited Los Angeles and said it was beautiful and exciting. Miles could use the break, his leg had been getting worse over the last year and Dr. Falk didn't seem to think it would get much better any time soon. But Miles was a stubborn man and kept working, despite her pleas for him to slow down. He rarely had time for fun these days. He didn't celebrate his birthday (though he always made a fuss for hers), he didn't care for Christmas, Easter nor Halloween. Not since his accident or the death of his father, Issac. He was more somber and just forgot about holidays really. Cathryn could remember Halloweens as a child being such a special time of the year. A time for mischief and magic. Even as she grew older, Cathryn couldn't let go of her inner child when she saw the pumpkins growing down on Mr. Brown's farm on the other side of town. But she could also remember just ten years back when she and Miles would celebrate all the holidays together, parties, drinking, costumes, Jack-O'-Lanterns, the whole nine yards. She wished she could help him more but she knew Miles and she knew time would help sooth him, at least mentally.

For now, there was the scarecrow, gently swaying in the breeze. A touch of spookiness on their farm. Everyone should have a little bit of creepiness on Halloween, have a bit of a fright or even a pumpkin carved into a scary face to mock the spirits.

Cathryn felt frustrated and sad.

'Maybe we'll have a good Halloween again one day.' She wished silently to the scarecrow.

She waited a moment to see if it would respond.

Nothing.

Cathryn sighed and went into the house to make dinner as the darkness came creeping over the fields.

The evening was uneventful but full of warmth. Miles and Cathryn shared two bottles of white wine over mozzarella stuffed chicken (Cathryn's favourite) and talked through into the evening, only taking a break to say hello to their nearest (half a mile away) neighbour Bruce Crane and his children, Henry and Charlotte, dressed in costumes.

"Wow, you two look great! A skeleton and a witch. Very scary!" Miles complimented, looking over their disguises.

"Thank you Mr. King!" The children said in unison, smiling up at him.

"Are you off trick or treating in town?" Miles asked.

Henry nodded silently and Charlotte, aged six, stepped forward. "We're gonna get lots of candy!"

Miles chuckled. "Well go inside, go see Cathryn and I'm sure you can scare a couple of sweet treats out of her."

He stepped aside and let the children in and turned back to Bruce.

"How's Ray doing?" Miles asked.

Bruce waved a hand. "Ah, Dad is okay. I think he's enjoying staying with us, bit more company for him. Him and Henry spent hours today carving pumpkins. He seems happy."

"That's good to hear."

They fell silent, hearing Cathryn's laughs from inside and Charlotte giving a wicked cackle.

"Is it workin'?" Bruce asked.

"What?" Miles asked puzzled.

Bruce pointed to the scarecrow.

"Oh, the scarecrow? Yeah…it's…well yeah it's working really well I suppose…stopping the birds. Thanks for it."

"Thanks for what?"

"The scarecrow," Miles replied.

"I didn't put it there," Bruce said.

*

The scratching noise came quietly.

Cathryn awoke, straining to hear the sound in her daze. She looked at the clock on the bedside table. It read 3:03 a.m, the soul's midnight, but the clock did not tick nor tock. She lifted her head from the pillow and listened. Maybe a mouse in the attic? A bird maybe flew in an open window? Or maybe it was a tree scrapping the house? No…there were none near the house and Miles had cleaned up and sealed the attic up just last month.

The sound was like a broom being dragged outside in the hallway or the sound made when Grandma used to beat down the rugs for dust.

The noises chilled Cathryn.

"I hear it too," Miles said quietly in the dark as he pulled himself up. The scratching continued as he mentally mapped out the layout of his home. The upstairs hallway had stairs at one end and their bedroom at the other, with three rooms in between.

Miles fumbled for the bedside lamp but the click of the switch brought no light to the room. Cathryn tried hers, spilling her book onto the floor in the process. Nothing. No light.

BAM!

A thud at the door shattered the night.

Cathryn jumped back up against the headboard. Fear and uncertainty spread though Miles.

The telephone was downstairs.

Scarping on the door.

Miles put an arm across his wife and a finger to his lips then slowly slipped out the warm bed, putting his bare feet on the chilly wooden floor. The burglar would be checking out the other rooms:

Cathryn's art room, the book room and the bathroom. That left…their room.

The twinge in his leg was apparent but his leg hadn't woken up from the sleep as he searched the room, turning in each direction trying to make out any object he could use in the darkness. He needed a weapon.

There were little thuds. Nearly two dozen in a row, each followed by scarping. Miles listened carefully.

More than one person? He thought with worry and dread.

He stood steps from the door. The rustling became slower. It was nearly a minute before he realised he was holding his breath while sweat rolled down his forehead.

There was someone in his house and he had to protect Cathryn.

The scream of breaking glass.

The intruder was in the bathroom…though Cathryn had water glasses for brushes in her art room. He couldn't tell where the burglar was.

"Miles?" Cathryn cried with a dry whisper from the bed.

He held out a hand to signal her to stay quiet and tried to plan what to do next.

The chair!

There was the wooden chair next to the bedroom door. Taking extra care not to press his foot onto the squeaky floorboard between the bed and the door, Miles lifted the clothes piled on top of the chair and tossed them softly onto the bed then he slowly and delicately moved the chair across the floor. Slowly inch by inch he pulled it, clenching his teeth so tight he feared they would shatter. Every slight scrap the chair made hurt him, deep in his chest. His leg felt on fire now supporting his weight, he needed relief.

BANG! The door pounded inwards. Miles let out a cry then fell to his knee hard.

Without hesitating, he pulled the chair the final distance and jammed it under the door knob.

They were safe.

BANG! Like a giant fist on the door.

BANG! BANG! BANG!

Then a sound that turned Miles cold and made Cathryn gasp.

A giggle.

The intruder was giggling. Barely audible but somewhere in the dark, the intruder was mocking them. It sent shudders through Miles as lifted himself from the floor.

BANG!

Giggle.

BANG! BANG! BANG!

"What do they want?!" Cathryn screamed over the thuds.

Miles felt the panic brewing within him when the silence hit.

It had stopped…not a sound from behind the door.

Miles and Cathryn both held their breaths waiting, neither daren't move.

The silence was cold and hard.

*

The couple remained relatively frozen for at least an hour (at least Miles imagined it was only an hour, it felt like eight) with no more noise from behind the door.

The breeze hit his foot.

It was coming through the small gap between the floor and bottom of the door. The front door was open downstairs letting in the wind, Miles deduced.

Something tickled his foot, just like a spider crawling across it. He bent slowly, not taking his eyes off the door, staying on the edge of the knife waiting for more sound. His own hand hitting his foot startled him but he bit his lip to keep the cry in.

Still no sound.

His fingers fumbled in the darkness and found a small pile of it, he knew exactly what it was.

"Straw," he whispered.

In an instant, orange light poured in from under the door, creating ghastly shadows across the back wall, distorting Miles' view of Cathryn.

The glow danced across the room.

"Is...what's the..." Miles tried to tell her.

Cathryn slid out of bed, her feet as light as a feather and walked toward the door, kneeling down in front of her husband, their heads nearly touching.

"Is there anything?" she whispered.

"I don't hear anything," Miles said, dropping the straw.

"Is it fire?" she asked worried, looked down at the flickering light.

Miles pushed a hand to the door. No heat. No smoke. He shook his head.

They bent down slowly, pressed their cheeks to the floor and peered under the door into the light.

Cathryn let out a gasp and shot back up.

Miles slowly rose and wiping the cold sweat from his brow. He stood, ignoring the dull pain in his leg.

He removed the wooden chair and opened the door.

The hallway was lined with Jack-O'-Lanterns! All shapes and sizes, colours and every kind of horrible and scary. Some stood proud and large among smaller ones and others were stacked three or four high. All the glowing faces peered up at the couple as they stepped out their bedroom, each pumpkin with a mocking laugh or a spooky grimace. Dotted between the pumpkins, standing like soldiers, were corn stalks. so many that it was difficult to see the wallpaper.

Miles took Cathryn's hand and walked toward the stairs, following the trail of straw strewn across the floor. The couple felt like strangers in their own home. The lanterns continued down the stairs. Misshapen pumpkin eyes followed the couple as they reached the living room where their strange audience glowed, burning bright, waiting for them on all possible surfaces.

Cathryn could smell pumpkin pie, drifting from somewhere in the house.

Miles' eyes followed the straw trails to the front door which stood wide open letting in the night wind.

He took a brave step outside and in the moonlight saw the straw leading down the porch steps, across the clearing and into the tall corn crop, which rustled with movement as something ran toward the distant woodland at the edge of the farm.

The cross of dead branches stood empty.

LITTLE STUFFED TIGERS

If there was one person in the town of Port Hampton people disliked and tried best to pretend didn't live there, it was one Frederick 'Ricky' Palmer.

Palmer, who had made his fortune from a lucky case of a dead father's will, had hunted animals all over the world and wasn't shy to brag about it. He drove through the streets in his giant off road sports jeep blaring country music at full volume, never obeying the speed limit unless a police car loomed nearby. He wore boots of crocodile skin and jackets trimmed with the pelts of his so called 'trophies' as he strutted with that smug grin on his face with a black cowboy hat covering his bald head.

"Now, you! Listen here right, let me tell you about this one time I shot this giraffe right between its eyes…" he would slur in his American drawl after a few too many double whiskies at 'The Fox & The Pheasant' to anyone near him. "Boy! She went down quick! Timber! What?! Ain't it funny for ya?"

His nights at the pub usually ended with the bartender kicking him out for being rowdy and likely to cause a fight, though, with his high priced lawyer behind him Palmer was untouchable during a fight, wither he started it or not, unless of course you were Mr. Tom York who broke Palmer's nose during a bar scuffle and was taken to court. Tom later said it was worth it).

Palmer lived at the top of Pershing Hill, on the east side of town, in a house paid for with blood money. It was a sprawling ranch style house, no doubt a replica of a house he owned back in his homeland in some southern state.

He had kept security tight.

Activists and animal lovers were often found protesting outside the house, usually peacefully but there had been incidents. Some leaving angry and hateful things on Palmer's doorstep. The things some of these people said they'd do to him made Palmer chuckle. He didn't care, take the scum to court. 'Bleed 'em dry' that was his motto, though…he had a firearm licence and a dozen rifles and shotguns in the house, all loaded, and he'd sure as Hell blow someone away if they tried entering his house.

Yes sir, blow 'em away.

The most hated man in town.

*

It was dark by 5:40pm when he exited the shower and stood air drying. Through his large wall sized window in the master bedroom, he could see parents taking their little kiddies out begging for candy dressed like stupid fools. Those silly Brits always stealing Halloween away from good

Americans. 'Britain is great,' his advisors back in the states had told him when he decided to move for 'accounting' reasons.

"Yeah, Britain is great, just full of the damn British," he muttered aloud to the empty bedroom.

The sound of the brewing storm was coming closer to town.

A woman herding children below looked up at Palmer from the street and appear shocked. He bellowed a laugh and shook his naked flabby body from side to side as she hurried the children along.

He wrapped his Egyptian cotton bathrobe over his damp body and went downstairs.

This was where he liked to relax.

The study.

The middle of the room was clear of all furniture and gave enough space for entertaining clients, streetwalkers and the few people he cared to call friends. He had furnished the room with dark mahogany all over; bookshelves (though Palmer had no time for books, he had had enough of them in school), a grand desk made of the material dominated the corner where he did all his business. The same wood, highly polished, was panelled on all four walls.

Expensive. It looked and smelled expensive.

The floor was covered with a deep shag ivory coloured carpet. It had to be cleaned every week by the maid to get his boot stains and the spilled booze out but damn did it cost a lot of money.

Nice and expensive. It felt luscious under his bare feet.

Palmer dropped down into one of the overstuffed red leather arm chair, clutching a tumbler of whisky and ice and faced toward his pride and joy.

His trophies.

Mounted on hand cut and sanded dark stained teak plaques were the two dozen animal heads calling out to him in silent roars, caws and growls. They might have been kings of their world or the respected leader of their packs but oh no, when Palmer had that heavy rifle in his hand, they became just another furry thing to put on his wall. They were just something else for him to point out to his buddies and claim he conquered. He chuckled at the thought, looking up at the head of the baby elephant (The tracking band said her name had been Ada), third from the left. He had hit the beast with a shot straight through her right eye from four hundred yards, he was proud of her.

Below her, a pair of bengal tigers, brother and sister (six months old the guide had told him when they found them somewhere in Japan, China or Asia, it was all the same to Palmer.) Two clean shots to the chest, couldn't even see the wound on the mounts. The two tigers, full body mounts as opposed to just the trophy heads, were rested on a log, standing in the far corner looking out into the centre of the room and now, in the warm light of the study, they looked even better as an accessory to match the tiger pelt throw on the sofa. Next to the sibling tigers, a lion, king of his pack. Palmer had hunted the big cat with a rich dentist named Rogers. They had to lure it out of the sanctuary with the help of some poor locals in need of money. Sure there were laws and all that but like one lion mattered. It was a long forty hours drawing the big cat out into the open but it had been pure euphoria when Palmer finally pulled the trigger and watched the lion breath its last breath.

Next to the lion, a wild boar, just a hog he had came across while driving and shot with a handgun out the car window, then a giraffe, a crocodile (he had the rest of the reptile's skin used for his boots and ate its meat), a prized swordfish from a trip he took with a couple of clients. Buffalo, antelope, wildebeest, gorilla, zebra, rhino (with full horn). So many animals, so many stories. Palmer had so many mounts he struggled sometimes to remember where and how he had hunted them. They were proof, solid proof, he was a man and man was the greatest animal on earth.

Each of these beasts he had brought down himself, hunted for days, stalked them and waited until the moment was right…then with a pull of a trigger, they belonged to him.

Mr. Lutz, the town taxidermy enthusiast, may be a wimp with his 'roadkill only' rule but Lutz was like rest of them, dirt poor and buyable. Five kids and a second wife don't come cheap. All Palmer had to do was wave little wad of cash (a small bunch of fun coupons for Palmer) under Lutz's nose and Lutz would hang his head and accept the job without eye contact. Damn animal lovers…To Hell with 'em.

Palmer gulped the last of his third whisky then, realising the ice bucket in the study was empty, walked into the kitchen.

Just like the study, he had spent a lot of money making the kitchen expensive. The gleaming grey marble counters were polished to a high sheen so clean and spotless you could eat the Kobe beer steaks in the refrigerator straight off them. All the most expensive kitchen tools and implements, thought he never used any of it. That's what the maid was for.

Pulling open the double door refrigerator, Palmer plucked the ice tray from the top shelf. Always three ice cubes. The delicate clink of the ice hitting the bottom of the glass was smothered by the thunder claps outside and the slowly at first but then hard hitting rain. The storm was now well over town and likely to last the night. He laughed out loud thinking about all those little kiddies getting soaked and crying. The more he pictured them the harder he laughed, his gut jiggling under his bathrobe.

He was so hysterical with laughter that he didn't even notice when the lights went out, surrounding him in dark in an instant. It was thick and he couldn't see a thing.

"Jesus H. Christ!" Palmer cursed.

There was no light coming from the window. It must be a town wide power cut or at least his block.

He yanked open the fridge but no light. The Kobe beef steaks would spoil and there would be Hell to pay if they did.

The drawer next to the fridge had matches in it but when he found the box, its rattle was weak and quiet.

The whisky bottle was in his hand when the low growl began and in a hundred sharp shards on the heated tiled floor when it quietened.

It had been low but there and he had heard enough growls during his business to know one when he heard one.

He daren't move.

It was those goddamn hippies with that mutt of theirs, that police type of dog. They had been parked at the bottom by his driveway the day before, playing their crappy songs on a guitar they probably stole, begging for pennies, eating their vegan rabbit food. Scum. They climbed the goddamn fence! He knew he should have installed that razor wire on top of all the fences and gates when he moved in but the neighbours had cried about hurting little birds or something.

Breaking and entering, that's a serious crime in Palmer's book and that whisky had gotten him in the mood to give a rifle a little go, dog or hippy.

He tried to shake the matches out the box but his chunky fingers only felt a single match. He cursed as he realised how difficult things were in the dark. If he could get to the study at least there was a flashlight in the desk and enough firepower to take down an army.

It was a mistake to take a step. The shattered glass ripped into the bottom of his foot, sending white hot pain up his leg. With a yelp he dropped the matchbox and clutched his foot with both hands. The glass had sunken deep but he could feel the exposed end of the shard puncture his palm.

There was another growl in the dark as he felt both his foot and hand get moist and warm with blood.

His anger level peaked.

"You! In there! Come out here and I'll blow ya head off!" he yelled, knowing full well he was lying.

No guns in the kitchen.

Dropping his hurt foot back to the floor was another mistake. The alcohol stung the wound, making him clench his yellowing teeth together. He cursed in the dark.

There was movement in the study.

Palmer tried to remember if he had locked the front door when he came back from the bar but he couldn't even remember arriving home. There was a trickle of sweat down the back of his red neck.

"Hey? You not hear too good?" he called out, trying to hide his pain.

No response.

He listened closely. He thought of the dog. The same breed the police used. Those Nazi dogs.

"You here doggie?"

Silence. If that mutt came in, he'd have to swing his legs and arms pretty hard to hurt it. Smash the mongrel against the counter before it could sink its teeth into him. Palmer was fit enough to whip anyone in this jerkwater town, why not a stupid dog?

He lifted a foot and sheepishly tried to take a step forward but screamed as a shard of the bottle sliced deep into his heel like a hot knife through butter. All his muscles contracted and pulsated at once. A jolt in his chest.

Another growl.

"Goddamn…"

In blind panic, Palmer swung an arm out to the counter, hoping to grasp at the Italian handmade and sharpened knife block (very expensive).

It was his third mistake of the evening, the sudden movement threw him off balance and he tumbled to the floor, grinding his whole body into the littered glass. The pain soared through his body like brutal acupuncture, feeling it hit every nerve.

"Get out of my house!" he screamed out trying to take the agony. The feeling of pumping blood gushed from every wound.

A growl. This time closer…in the kitchen.

Palmer groped blindly in front of him when his fingers reached, among the glass, the dropped match. Quickly he struck it with his thumbnail and the soft circle of light revealed the extent of his injuries.

Blood streaked all over his hands and forearms. The once white bathrobe stained crimson. The fall had driven glass into the bottom of his chins. Keeping his head low, he spat blood to the floor and saw the mixture of whisky and his own fluids mix.

He breathed deep, feeling his own breath bounce back up from the floor to his face…then he

felt the warm breath on the top of his bald head…
then another breath on his left ear.

And slowly raising his head, with the circle of
the light diminishing as the match began to burn out,
he could see them.

Four paws.

Orange, black and white paws with sharp
claws.

Despite his screams reaching the ears of a few
trick or treaters at the bottom of Pershing Hill, the
adult neighbours would later claim they never heard a
sound.

*

Officer Horton stood, nursing a hangover, in
the kitchen looking around with fuzzy eyes. Though
the blood had been sprayed across the room, he could
tell that it had been a new and very expensive refit, all
new appliances and work surfaces.

Looking down, Horton followed the blood
trail, caused by the victim dragging himself along the

once shining white tiles through into the adjoining study, which Horton stepped into and glanced at what was left of Mr. Frederick Palmer, a well known resident of the town (though from interviews with neighbours he learnt not a well liked resident). The ivory carpet was sodden with the man's blood and stomach fluids, such a shame for a luxury carpet like this. The county coroner had come, gone and confirmed what Horton had suspected. A dog attack. The front gate had been left open and the main door had been left unlocked…a dog must of wandered in or been set on Palmer. The man had enemies for sure, Horton had seen and broken up several protests at the bottom of the hill before. A big dog the coroner had speculated. Horton knew of Derek and Laura Simpson, two of Port Hampton's less desirable residents and Palmer protesters who lived the hippy, free spirit life in an old orange VW van, a rust bucket on wheels. The couple kept a German Shepherd named Spud, which had bitten the hand of a toddler just two days ago.

That would be his first port of call, Horton thought as he left the room and walked out into the early morning air.

As the day wound down, the detectives left, Palmer's remains were taken to the mortuary and the house was sealed and fell silent.

But no one on the scene noticed the blood on the claws and teeth of the little stuffed tigers in the corner of the study.

A JACK-O'-LANTERN TALE

Though it was dark and she had been told to wait inside, Maya Fox sat on the porch, clutching her small pumpkin, looking out to the street waiting for her mother to return. It was 5:30pm and the shops would now be closed. She hoped her mother, who the adults called Dawn, had gotten it. It was perfect when she saw it, on the Monday before last, she fell in love with it but her mother had said she would have to wait until the pennies came at the end of the month. Maya had learnt from a young age that the pennies came at the end of the month, one part from Mummy's cleaning job and the other part from the post office book (and sometimes Grandma helped out with the rent).

The other kids on the block had started trick or treating, not many, but mostly the younger babies and being now nine years old, Maya considered herself not a baby. The real trick or treating wouldn't start until about 7:00pm but before that could happen she needed two things: a costume and a Jack-O'-Lantern.

The bus arrived at the end of the street and Dawn stepped off clutching grocery bags. Maya's heart jumped as she stood, heaving the pumpkin against her chest.

"Hi Sweetie," Dawn smiled up with her work apron still on under her parka coat.

"Did you get it Mummy?"

Dawn sighed and looked down at her tired feet. "I'm sorry baby, not enough pennies this month for the cat one."

Though Maya was young, she knew her mother hated saying that sentence.

"Remember we need to fix the hot water? So you can have normal baths again," Dawn explained.

Maya nodded and felt disappointment but didn't want her mother to see it.

Dawn sat down on the porch steps and put the grocery bags between her feet. Maya could smell the cleaning solution on her mother's apron, some said it was an ugly harsh smell but to Maya it was comforting, it let her know her mother was home again.

"But you know what? I got…" Dawn began, feeling her heart sink at the sad eyes of her daughter. "I got you this," she said with a smile handing Maya one of the bags.

Peering in with curiosity, Maya pulled out the bag's contents.

A black witches hat, adorned with silver and gold spider webs of glitter all across the wide brim. Spooky drawings of cats, pumpkins, stars and moons wrapped around the cone.

With her other hand, she pulled a simple black cape with the same glitter patterns.

A matching set.

"This was on sale in 'Taylor's'. I know it's not the cat but a witch is even better don't you think?" Dawn asked, flattening out the cape on her lap. Her daughter sat silent for a moment and Dawn felt, for a moment just as long, like a failure. She always tried to make her daughter happy but there was always an emergency that came up just as the pay cheque came in. Last month it was black mould, this month it was a broken boiler.

The moment passed when Maya gave a delighted squeal and her beautiful smile (though missing a few baby teeth) spread across her face.

"I love it!"

And putting the pumpkin onto the porch next to her, Maya reached over and hugged her mother tightly. Dawn felt a wave of relief and enjoyed the embrace.

Maya completely forgot about the cat costume.

After Dawn had taken off her shoes and hung her apron, she and Maya put away the groceries, then had a simple dinner of spaghetti before sitting down to carve the pumpkin.

It was a small one, just the right size for Maya to hold by herself. Dawn guided her daughter's little hand with the little plastic saw they had gotten last year and the lid of the developing lantern came free. Squishing and squelching her hands, Maya pulled the innards out and dropped them into the bowl next to her. There was nothing quite like feeling all the seeds and stringy bits between her fingers.

It was a pleasure only allowed in October.

"We'll bake these too. They're very tasty," Dawn said, picking the white almond shape seeds from the mush.

With the candle inside, the grimacing face shone brightly. Maya had chosen, maybe not the scariest face but a face she felt represented Halloween as a whole.

Two triangle eyes, a smaller triangle nose and a smile with three crooked teeth. Maya felt pride in her creation.

At 7:00pm, it was finally trick or treating time. Maya had donned her costume and was ready to go out into the night and cast her spell over the town.

In the living room, she could hear a Halloween special on the television but was unsure if it was a Disney or a Looney Tunes special.

"Mummy?" Maya asked, walking into the living room.

Dawn was on the sofa, gently snoring, exhausted and asleep.

Without thinking, anger or annoyance, Maya lifted the blanket off the side chair under the window and draped it over her mother. It was nice to see her so peaceful, usually she was so stressed and worried about things. School might be six whole hours but she knew her mother worked almost twice that every day.

Dawn shifted, a subtle smile crossed her face and she slept.

Taking the spare house key, the one on the yellow string, Maya tied it around her neck and tucked it under her dress. She would only go up and down the street, she knew everyone who lived in the little cul-de-sac.

She pulled a paper bag from the kitchen drawer and with a marker pen wrote in big blue letters: '*Trick 'r Treat'*.

She pulled up her Jack-O'-Lantern and headed for the front door. Her mother could sleep for an hour or so and Maya would return with a bag full of candy in time to watch *It's The Grand Pumpkin, Charlie Brown* later that night, maybe Mummy would be awake for that. They could share candy.

The outside had that feel, that feel that only came on Halloween (Christmas was just as good, but a very different feeling). It was supernatural, uncanny and special.

Though Maya had friends at school, they were not allowed to trick or treat. Their parents thought it was a silly thing to go and do. They stuck to pumpkin carving and Halloween television specials. But how could you celebrate Halloween without the age old tradition of trick or treat? You had to trick or treat on the last day of October, it was Halloween law, you had to!

Bumbling down the steps and out the front gate, Maya began to walk toward the end of the street, start at one end and work down each house, only the houses with Jack-O'-Lanterns or decorations were to be knocked on was Mummy's rule.

Some adults didn't care for Halloween, a thought that upset Maya.

Up and down the street, she could see the other kids, some were spacemen, some were monsters, vampires, werewolves, Frankenstein, bedsheet ghosts, zombies, ghouls, firemen. All sorts. No other night of the year could you see such wondrous sights.

*

Maya had been to eight of the houses on the cul-de-sac, missing out Mr. Kreeg's house which stood with no decorations or any Halloween spirit. She had filled half of her little paper bag with candy. Some houses gave little bags of gummy sweets and others gave full sized chocolate bars, the good stuff (Mrs. Myers at number 34 was giving out white chocolate, Mummy's favourite).

It was just before she reached the alley, the one connecting Proctor Street and her cul-de-sac, St Helena Way, that Kelly Krug called out from the shadows.

"Oi, Maya!"

The call made Maya's heart sink like a stone.

Kelly Krug was a bully and she picked on everyone at Maya's school. Kelly stole from school bags and the teacher's desk, took milk money and every lunch break was looking over your shoulder incase Kelly came prowling, looking for someone to push around.

"What you got there huh?" Kelly moved forward. Her dirty sand coloured hair, stuck up like a pineapple and her loud mouth smeared with chocolate. "You got sweets? You been out begging again?"

Maya took a step back and stole a quick glance over her shoulder. Her house was at the other end of the street and the street now stood vacant with no sign of other kids.

"No…well…It's trick or treating…" Maya began, rearranging the pumpkin under her arm.

"No, you beg! You been out dipping your scummy hands into candy you can't afford," Kelly

mocked then spat down at Maya's feet. "Gimme it!"
Saliva still swinging from her chin.

Though Maya clutched the paper bag tightly,
Kelly was too quick. With one swoop of her thick
arm, Kelly shoved Maya against the fence. She tried to
protect her pumpkin and her free hand hit the
ground, grazing against the gravel and grit of the
alley. Maya let out a cry as tears began to form in her
eyes but she couldn't let Kelly see them.

"Mine now!" Kelly claimed, dumping the
stolen paper bag into her own dirty pillow sack bag.
The bully raised a fist and lent down to Maya's face,
the threat of a punch made Maya wince.

Kelly swiped the witches hat from Maya's
head.

"No!" Maya cried, trying to stand quickly, her
hurt hand reaching out for the hat.

Kelly planted a foot against the front of
Maya's dress and pushed her back to the ground.

The Jack-O'-Lantern fell and extinguished.

"Tell your mum that she didn't clean our bathroom good so my mum ain't gonna pay her!" Kelly gave a final taunt, tossing Maya a single lollypop and waddled out into Proctor Street and around the corner wearing the glittery witches hat.

As she inspected her palm, seeing the familiar red and black graze from learning to ride a bike, Maya tried to keep her tears in but the feeling in her stomach made her sick. She didn't want to cry for her hand, though it hurt, it was tears coming over wasted pennies. Kelly had taken the hat Mummy had bought for her and it might as well have been a bar of solid gold to Maya. Mummy had worked hard for it and Maya had stupidly let it be taken, just because Kelly was going to punch her (And she had felt the bully's punch before). Maya would go home and Mummy would wake up and see no hat and a ripped cape and be so upset and…and…

As the tears flowed, the alley became distorted and watery. Things blurred and blended together creating illusions that tricked the mind.

Like the pumpkin, now sitting still in front of her, which gave her a soothing feeling of calm that, although comforting, didn't quite overflow and smother the guilt and sense of shame.

The pumpkin's triangle eyes watched the sad girl.

Suddenly, grey smoke rose from inside its mouth and the candle within burst to life, the flame licking the goofy teeth and giving its eyes life and then, a tear induced trick of the mind, the pumpkin winked at her. A single playful wink that caught Maya's breath and temporarily stopped the crying.

Before she could quite process what the pumpkin had done, it began to roll away from her, out of the alley and around the corner into the street.

When Maya finally stood and peered around the corner into Proctor Street, both Kelly and the pumpkin were nowhere in sight.

*

Dropping her heavy foot into every Jack-O'-Lantern that came in her path, Kelly was nearly halfway home when she started eating. She had taken the candy of maybe eleven or twelve kids along her journey. Each kid had given their bags over after a punch or two or, even like baby Maya Fox, just holding up a fist was enough to get their haul. Kelly giggled at the thought and continued wolfing down a caramel bar. She could go home and feast all she wanted now. She wasn't going to go door to door and beg when it was so easy just to take it from the babies and no way was she going to actually go buy some candy!

Plod. Plod. Plod.

She reached into her pillow sack for another chocolate bar, all the more sweeter for being free and taken from the little babies, when she heard the sound.

Plod. Plod. Plod.

Turning, she saw only the empty street, the cars still and houses lit up. The trick or treaters had died out now and Kelly knew that the big kids would come out soon. The ones in middle school. It was best to get home before they came out causing trouble.

Plod. Plod. Plod.

Kelly scoffed and kept walking quickly. It was getting cold and the wind was starting to blow a storm, making her hold a dirty hand on her new witches hat to stop it getting swept away with the dead leaves. She looked forward to laying in bed eating all the candy, giggling at the losers and their Halloween.

Stopping in her tracks, she punctuated the gleeful thought with another kick to a Jack-O'-Lantern.

Plod. Plod. Plod.

She stood still.

Again, she turned looking for the noise, looking down the footpath between the parked cars and houses.

Nothing.

Plod. Plod. Plod.

Stepping off the curb and across the street, she caught a quick flash disappear down the side alley between two dark houses, an overgrown little trail leading to the garages.

It was there, in the middle of the path, she saw a Jack-O'-Lantern.

It was no bigger than her head. It had stupid triangle eyes and a stupid goofball smile with three teeth.

Perfect for smashing.

"Kelly…" The wind whispered.

The sound made her hesitate, just for a second, breaking the momentum of her leg as she swung it toward the pumpkin. She glanced up at the rattle of leaves falling from the vacant trees above her then yelped loudly at the pain in her shin.

The pumpkin had swallowed her whole foot and now looked up at her like a shoe with menace. Its goofy teeth spread and stretched, working their way up her leg. She could see her own blood. The teeth were firm, feeling like a table vice clamped on her leg. The absurdity of the situation stopped her screaming, unable to realise what was happening, even as the pumpkin started to grow, growing in size to accommodate her limb. It was clawing its way up further and further, past her knee…up to her thigh, working its way to her hip. The pumpkin bulged and contorted, its animated mouth gnawing up closer and closer. Her leg felt wet and mushy but it was hot. Hot like the fire burning in the Jack-O'-Lantern's wicked eyes, the fire that grew and seeped out from the pumpkin's features shining terror across Kelly's face. The strange fruit grew and grew, swallowing each part of her, teeth breaking her bones, pulling her further and further in. Every swing of her heavy arms was futile. The pumpkin clawed up past her waist, her chest then it swallowed her head, sucking in her arms until there was nothing left.

The flames within the pumpkin burned bright and hot as an oven.

The roar of the fire covered the screams of Kelly Krug.

*

It's The Grand Pumpkin, Charlie Brown would be starting in less than ten minutes. Maya knew this because she could hear the announcements on the television inside as she sat on the porch steps just as she had done earlier that night. Mummy was still asleep. Maya wished to the October night that Mummy wouldn't be disappointed with her and that her and Mummy could be happy to enjoy the night. She had been told that anything was possible on Halloween, that wishes came true and the spirits would help people in need. Maya wanted to believe the stories. She had lost her hat, her candy and her pumpkin.

A lost Halloween.

She had to be a big girl and not cry anymore.

She rested her chin on her sore hand and sighed closing her eyes. She thought of the next school day and having to see Kelly, having to see how Kelly would laugh and point, making fun of her. Dread filled Maya's stomach, which was hungry for candy that only taste good on Halloween night.

It was the thud that made her open her eyes.

At the foot of the gate, the size of the big blue armchair in the living room, sat the Jack-O'Lantern.

Her Jack-O'-Lantern.

The pumpkin had the same silly face as she had carved with Mummy. But now…now it looked almost satisfied, like the kind of face Grandma made after a good meal.

Now with clear eyes she knew it wasn't an illusion. The pumpkin winked again and its smile spread with the flame glowing warmly inside and suddenly from the giant happy mouth, out poured candy, spilling from the flames unsinged, unconcerned and unburnt. Maya stood in awe, watching all the different labels, sizes and types of candy collect at her feet. It was a weeks, maybe a months, worth of candy. She would share it with everyone she knew at school.

Then from the pumpkin's mouth, sweeping along the flowing candy like a paper boat on water, rode Maya's witches hat and it came to a gentle stop at her feet. Picking it up, Maya allowed her tears, now tears of joy and disbelief, to flow freely as she placed the hat upon her head.

With utter thanks and love, Maya fell forward and gave the Jack-O'-Lantern the biggest hug she could muster, feeling its warmth all across her body, cheek and hands.

Her innocent tears trickled down its smooth orange flesh.

"Thank you," she said in a delicate whisper.

And the pumpkin said, "you're welcome."

SPOOKHOUSE

"It's everything you imagine! Gore, blood, pus and organs!" Hunter Weiss squealed full of delight as he and Stephen Frost ran across the field in the shadow of the Port Hampton castle ruins toward the admission gate.

"You been in it?" Stephen asked, trying to keep up pace.

"No but Robin and Humphrey told me it was brilliant! It's a SpookHouse."

Stephen knew that meant it was scary, something he wasn't overly fond of feeling but he was tired of the other boys making fun of him.

The fair had arrived only two days before, on the 29th, during the dark October night with no warning, announcement or invitation so that the town people could discover it in the morning like fresh dew. There were nearly two dozen brightly coloured canopies circled with strings of Edison bulbs glowing dimly attracting the moths. The smell of popcorn, hot dogs (which Stephen hoped for as Hunter had made him skip dinner) and soda pop swam in the air. An organ played a cheerful tune somewhere inside the maze of sideshows and stalls.

The two boys joined the line of eager people pushing their coins across the counter in exchange for a paper ticket stub from the strange looking Carny.

Hunter dug deep into his pocket, withdrew his money and lint, then pushed a hand towards the widely smiling man behind the counter.

"What'll it be boy?" the carny drawled happily, holding out his arms.

"One please!" Hunter requested gleefully.

Stephen looked at the carny and felt slightly unwell. The man wore a flat straw boater hat that had seen better days and a burgundy pinstripe jacket. The carny clutched a long cigar in his hand. His crooked brown teeth smiled down on the boys.

"Why of course, here for the elephants? Or maybe the clowns?"

"No, we want to see the spookhouse!" Hunter explained.

"Ah you're one of those morbid and macabre boys hey? Here to see murder and mayhem hey?" the carny chuckled. "Well I suppose you might like to see ol' Elmer…"

The carney handed down a ticket to Hunter who pushed through the gate into the carnival with his eyes darting in every direction.

A wooden cane fell on Stephen's shoulder.

"Tell me boy, how old are you?" the carny took a puff on his stinky cigar.

"Twelve." Stephen replied dryly.

The carny rubbed his bristled chin with the wet end of the cigar. "What's ya name?"

"Ste…Stephen." The anxiety was rising in Stephen's throat.

"Parents know you here?"

"Yes." Stephen lied, trying to look for Hunter on the other side of the gate.

"Stephen…Stephen…" the carny quietly repeated then, with a quick glance around to make sure they were alone, snorted and spat a brown blob on the floor next to Stephen's foot.

The carny reached across the counter for a ticket. Stephen quickly pulled out his coins and thrust them into the carny's hand. The chewed nicotine yellow fingers made Stephen want to retch and flee but he reached out and snatched the ticket from the carny's hand then ran through the gate into the crowd looking for warmth.

"It's somewhere around here…" Hunter insisted, after pushing his way through the tall adults for nearly ten minutes. Most of the older boys there were busy trying to impress girls at the shooting gallery or the game where you lift the hammer over your head and slam it down to hit the bell, the game Stephen wasn't strong enough for.

"The Hall of Mirrors is over that way," Hunter shouted over the surrounding laughs and cheers. "I think it's back this way. We haven't looked there. Come on."

The two turned in the opposite direction and after a few minutes, between the towering Helter Skelter and something called 'The Mystery Spot' (a tent that both intrigued and scared Stephen) they found it.

The SpookHouse was painted black as night, its wooden walls splintering and warped in places. It looked like it had travelled to a thousand and one different carnivals. There were paintings, though very basic, of movie monsters like Dracula and Frankenstein and even Gill-Man. The sight of gallows sticking out high above of the door gave Stephen a chill. The noose in the cold wind swayed in sync with his heartbeat. The heavy door was held on with rusted iron hinges.

"No line! Must be rubbish. Maybe Robin and Humphrey were lying," Hunter shrugged, taking a few steps closer. He stared at the red gothic looking words around the door and read out load.

Shudder at the bloody massacre.
Feel your blood chill as you gaze at the grotesque sights!
View the shocking collection of terror!
Dare you witness the madness within?

Stephen took a gulp and wiped the sweat from his palms on his jeans.

"Sounds fun!" Hunter said cheerfully.

It sounded like Hell for Stephen.

Hunter must of seen his fear.

"What's wrong now crybaby? You scared?" Hunter mocked.

"I…No. I can do it," Stephen said, hoping his voice wouldn't squeak like it had been the last month.

"Well…come on then!" Hunter pointed to the door.

Stephen could feel the familiar feeling of heavy feet and weak knees. The fear. But he couldn't let the fear get to him. Not again.

"Come on Stephen, don't be a complete baby."

It took all of Stephen's might to walk across the dying grass to the large door. It swung inward with a grinding creak and the musty blackness swallowed them both.

Inside they found themselves in a corridor. A scratchy sound effect record full of repeated screams and howls played somewhere on echoing speakers fixed on the ceiling. The walls were decorated with faded bats and skulls painted probably a hundred years ago.

Hunter walked ahead full steam toward the curtain made of ragged strips of cloth and disappeared into the next room, from which he gave a cry, a quick yelp that felt like a dagger in Stephen's chest, who tried to take a step forward but found himself rooted to the spot.

"What's takin' ya so long?" Hunter called back annoyed. "Come see this!"

Stephen questioned for a moment if he really wanted to see what Hunter was suggesting but found himself walking through the dirty rags.

The man gave Stephen a fright that hurt. Standing completely still in the room, the only thing in the room, was a man.

The man wore a dark suit two sizes too small, his ankles were on show and his shirt was yellowing with age and mould. The man's mouth was parted slightly in an awful groan, showing a black gap between his sets of teeth, big enough to fit a finger. In a clenched fist over his head, the man held a pair of large scissors, ready to stab.

Hunter scoffed. "It's just a stupid dummy."

He waved a hand at it and looked around for another door. "Where's the good stuff?"

Stephen pointed at the wall next to the dummy. "There's a sign."

"Meh, I ain't doing anymore reading," Hunter stated.

"*Here stands Mr. Elmer McCreedy, body snatcher and Necroph…*" Stephen squinted at the word but the type was faded. He skipped it and kept reading aloud. "*…A coin in the mouth…*"

The rest of the sign had faded and was unreadable.

Stephen shuddered. Hunter looked closer at the sign.

"A coin…a coin in the mouth. That's what it says," Hunter quickly dug into his pockets, pulling out bubble gum wrappers. He found a single coin. "Ah, last one. Maybe he'll do something!"

Without hesitation, as if it were a simple every day task, Hunter reached up and pushed the coin in McCreedy's open mouth with complete confidence then listened as it rattled down the throat before hitting, what Stephen assumed was, a box under the suit, where it clinked against other coins.

The two boys waited but nothing happened.

"Bah! What a rip!" Hunter gave the dummy a slap. "Not scary at all and he don't do nothin'."

Stephen felt the cold sweat on the back of his neck.

"He's boring. Not gory. Humphrey told me there was good stuff in here. That carny probably tricks everyone so he can get all the coins out of there at the end of the night."

Hunter lost interest and moved into the next room, leaving Stephen alone with McCreedy. Digging into every pocket while Elmer's glassy eyes watched on, Stephen looked for a coin. A peace offering of sorts but he couldn't find one. He has spent the last coin on his admission ticket. He quickly slunk away into the next room to follow Hunter.

McCreedy stood silent.

The next room was small, no bigger than four phone booths stuck together, just room enough for both boys to move around in.

It contained glass jars of various sizes on various shaped shelfs at various heights. It looked like a gruesome supermarket aisle. Each jar had a neat typewritten label affixed to it: Cancer of the liver, buckshot to left lung, heart of a child aged eight, the penis of a midget (which Hunter giggled at), brain of a lunatic. Diseases and illnesses pickled in jars for all to see. Things that were supposed to be on the inside of people not the outside. The things doctors were only suppose to see in real life…or morticians.

The sights were making Stephen feel unwell. He could hear the slices of a scalpel as these things were being removed from sick people. He could hear the patients screaming on an operating table. Where had these things even come from?

"Ah these weren't worth it. Let's go," Hunter dismissed with a tug of Stephen's shirt.

Who had gotten these jars? Why have them? Just for money? Just to show at little towns up and down the country for people to gawk at? It struck Stephen as a completely foreign idea.

He took one last spin around, looking at each of the slightly cloudy jars then went into the next room.

The sound effect record on repeat was starting to embed itself into Stephen's brain. The same four or five screams and maniacal laughs again and again. Like a trance designed to drive the listener insane.

The next room was empty, empty at least of people.

"Hun…Hunter?" Stephen stuttered to the corridor before him.

"It's boring in there. Just pictures," Hunter called from behind the curtain at the far end.

Stephen let his eyes rise to the crookedly hung portraits on the wall.

A wood etching of a bearded wild man, with crazy eyes, hunched on all fours with a baby in his mouth. He was eating the child.

The next painting was of the Grim Reaper, holding a scythe and a golden coloured hourglass filled with red sand. Behind the Reaper lay a barren dismal looking wasteland.

People in black and white outfits and hats with buckles on them holding torches up to a group of women standing in a fire (Stephen knew this was a witch burning, he had read about the ones that had happened in Port Hampton hundreds of years before).

A beautiful woman with her head in a guillotine. The large sharp blade raised high above her neck by a large man in a black hood.

Next, a black and white photo of…

"There's more this way but wow what a rip…" Hunter called back from somewhere.

…an electric chair with a handcuffed man being lead toward it by two prison guards. The handcuffed man looked haunted.

The next photograph was of the condemned man's execution. It made Stephen feel cold, ice cold. The man had a hood on and a hat with screws and thick wires coming out of it, his hands contorted like a cat's paws stretching. Stephen could almost hear the electricity.

A photograph of a black man hanging from a tree with a sea of white faces below the swinging body, some were smiling. The lynched man's face was bloated.

Stephen felt the queasiness build in his stomach. This was a mistake. Time to leave and get fresh night air. Hot dogs were now the last thing he wanted.

The last photograph took all the wind from Stephen's lungs and drained his face. He tried to speak, to utter any word to break the eerie silence, but nothing came.

It was a photograph of Elmer McCreedy.

McCreedy was laid out on a table in the suit two sizes too small and the same yellowed shirt. A group of somber looking men stood behind McCreedy, some dressed in black suits with black top hats and others in police uniforms. McCreedy's eyes stared right into Stephen's soul as the young boy felt his gaze drop to the little sign underneath the frame.

He read slowly, one word at a time…

'The corpse of Mr. Elmer McCreedy, body snatcher and necrophiliac. Died in New Orleans, Louisiana in 1952. Killed by Sargent Jerome (pictured) during a shoot out at St. Louis Cemetery No. 1. McCreedy's body was embalmed by the Hawthorne Mortuary but never claimed. His body was sold to the carnival circuit as 'The Ghoul of The Big Easy' and now stands in the lobby of the SpookHouse for all to see.

A coin in the mouth keeps McCreedy away.'

Stephen tried to breath steadily as the light began to fade above him but found he could not control his own bodily functions. Was it simply panic drowning out the light from his eyes or was the fear itself draining the safe light from the room?

It hadn't been a wax dummy or a shop mannequin.

A real life dead person.

A corpse.

A cadaver.

When the light finally died and Stephen felt the urine trickle down his leg, he heard the shuffling coming from the end of the corridor...slow...dragging...then it sped up...closer and closer and then Stephen could hear the unmistakable sound of coins jingling in the dark.

*

When Hunter returned to the SpookHouse with adults after hearing his friend's screams, none of them could find a single trace of young Stephen Frost...nor any sign of Elmer McCreedy.

THE AMBULANCE

The accident happened at 1:44pm in the afternoon on the 24th of October. The ambulance arrived at 1:50pm and took store manager Tim Taylor away. He had lost three fingers on the timber saw at 'Taylor's', the hardware store up near the Carnegie library. A freak accident.

"You ever see so much blood?" Randy Jones asked as he and Richard Campbell stepped back behind the counter to serve the line of customers.

"Nope and I hope I never do again," Richard replied, holding his stomach. "Enough to make you chuck your lunch."

"Man, I hope they can fix Tim up, poor guy," Randy said then continued to serve the next in line.

*

On the 25th, Mr. Aaron Hallums, over on Proctor Street, was raking the leaves in his garden with his head down and muttering to himself about the cold when he unknowingly stepped into a hidden hole his prized pug, Hamish, had dug the previous day. Hallums stumbled and fell onto a bush stump sticking up from the undergrowth, impaling his side just above the hip.

His wife Lydia had heard his cries and immediately dialled the phone for help at 2:00pm (The grandfather clock in the hallway was chiming as she pleaded for help) and the sound of the ambulance was heard outside their house at 2:04pm.

*

The next day at the 'Café Noir' across town, Kim Blair, aged twenty two, was making coffee for the early morning customers when her co-worker accidentally smashed the coffee pot against the counter, spraying searing hot coffee across Kim's head, chest and arms as she was bent down looking for more cups. Her wrist watch beeped 8:00am as she writhed on the floor in agony. A concerned customer called for help using the payphone just outside the café.

The ambulance arrived at 8:02am, despite the morning traffic.

*

On the 27th, at 6:00pm, Greg Burns was hit by a heavy weather vane blown from the roof of the house he walked by on Elizabeth Avenue. The wrong place at the wrong time. The owner of the house, Max Grierson, immediately called emergency services at the sight of the man bleeding profusely, a sight he caught by chance walking past his living room window. The right place at the right time.

The ambulance arrived at 6:01pm, just seconds after Max reached the injured man's side.

*

October 30th.

"These accidents are happening more and more these days," Lauren said, reading over the newspaper. "Lots of bad luck going around."

Ben Chandler sat looking out the window not hearing his wife's words. There had been no news about his friend Scott. He and Ben had been at 'The Fox & The Pheasant' in town two nights ago, celebrating Scott's upcoming boxing match. The American, Frederick Palmer, had tried to start a fight with the boxer but Scott, being a gentle man outside the ring, decided it best to just leave.

Scott hadn't been home since.

No one had seen or heard from him since leaving the bar. His wife Cat was sick with worry and filed a missing person report the previous night.

Lauren frowned over at her husband. He was doing that face, the face he made when he was mulling things over in his head. "No calls from Scott?"

Ben shook his head.

"I'm sure it's just a big misunderstanding, he'll be okay. He's a big fellow. Maybe he's got something planned for Cat? A surprise maybe?" Lauren suggested.

Ben couldn't believe his wife's casualness. He nodded simply but he was disagreeing.

After breakfast, Ben put Columbo, their eight year old Basset Hound, on his leash and went out into the morning. The ground was full of foliage with the mist making it feel damp under his boots as he scuffed them along the grassy field, letting Columbo sniff every bush and tree they passed.

Ben thought of the night at the pub. Had he noticed anything? Someone strange at the bar? A troublemaker? Scott hadn't been flashing cash or anything like some of the guys down there nor had Scott squared up to Palmer either. No trouble, no worries. They had talked with Randy Jones from

'Taylor's', who told them about his boss Tim losing half his hand in the timber saw.

Randy had seemed perplexed when describing the help that came.

"You shoulda' seen these paramedic guys man. White jackets and little hats, carrying this long stretcher. They came in, told us they had come for Tim…they came in see…" Randy had explained draining his beer then ordering another two. "They wrapped Tim's hand up in gauze then helped him up then put him in the back of the ambulance and drove off."

"Sounds normal. That's usually what paramedics do you know Randy, help people," Scott laughed with a hand on Randy's shoulder.

Randy shrugged, "I suppose. I mean, you didn't see these fingers. The saw flung 'em all over the store. Grisly mess. I just wanted to make sure Tim was okay so I followed them out the store…" Randy paused and looked at his bubbling glass. "But…you know, I didn't notice at first, maybe it was shock or something…but they they were driving a…what's the word? Vintage? Retro? Is that the word? It was an ambulance that looked like it was out of the 1950's or somethin'. Well then John Nash, you know the house painter, he told me he had seen the ambulance in the car park when he came into the store, like five minutes before Tim had his accident."

He finished his second beer.

Ben had stopped listening when Randy had mentioned the men in white and the ambulance and he had to admit it wasn't the first time he had heard, or seen, them or that ambulance. A few days ago, he had been at the 'Café Noir' when the barista was burnt with hot coffee. Ben had run outside to the payphone and called for help. It seemed like a long time but the young girl never stopped screaming. Ben shuddered at the memory of the girl's peeling and blistering skin but he helped her up and out into the street but even he failed to register it at first, just like

Randy hadn't. It was a long white car, almost like a hearse, with white wall tires and a blue rotating bubble light on top with big headlights, each door with a simple red cross on it. The men in white helped the girl into the back of the vehicle saying they were from a hospital. Ben had called an ambulance and one arrived. At the time he didn't think to question it over the young girls tear's.

*

When Ben returned home with Columbo, he knew something was wrong with his wife.

Lauren was at the sink staring out the window into the autumn garden.

"It's Greg…" she muttered, wiping a tear from her cheek.

Lauren worked with Greg Burns at the 'Scala' movie theatre, Greg as the co-manager (along with George Thompson) and Lauren as the supervisor. Greg was a pleasure to know and had recently had his first child with his wife Kate. He had a serious case of bad luck with an accident a few days before.

"He died. The theatre will be closed for a few days. George says…" and Lauren began to cry, unable to finish her sentence.

Once she had had a glass of wine and let the tears flow, she managed to talk as Ben sat with her.

"The weather vane I guess, just blew off the roof. It didn't…It just blew right off. It…Well you don't need to hear. Such a horrible thing to happen. Poor Greg…and Kate and Jennifer…oh no."

"What happened after he was…the accident?" Ben asked, Randy's story and the 'Café Noir' still fresh in his mind.

"Well…Max called an ambulance and then ran out to help Greg best he could," Lauren started, looking slightly puzzled.

"Did he mention anything about the ambul…?" he asked, not sure he wanted to know the answer.

"It's weird you mention that, Max said it was a strange…like a strange ambulance, like something from the 1950's."

*

It was the next day, Halloween, that Ben got the call.

Scott had been found and was in the hospital. For the past two days he had been unconscious and on pain medication after what appeared to be violent mugging.

It was Cat who called Ben.

"His wallet was taken, no ID. The doctors had no way of knowing. It was only when I called this morning asking and mentioned his boxing glove tattoo."

"And he's going to be okay?"

"Dr. Falk thinks so. It looks like someone had tried to treat him. His chest was bandaged but showed signs of infection."

"Do you know who found him?"

"No, no one knows. No one remembers admitting him."

Ben felt his stomach drop.

"What happened to him Ben?" Cat cried.

"When are visiting hours?" he asked quickly.

*

Port Hampton Memorial Hospital, a new modern building, sat at the bottom of a looming hill. It was overlooked by the gothic architecture of St. John's Psychiatric Hospital.

Upon reaching reception with a little over an hour left of visiting hours, Ben was directed to the third floor then to the third room on the left after the cafeteria.

Ben met Dr. Falk, who in basic terms, explained Scott's condition best he could.

Scott would live but it would be a lengthy recovery. There was still no light shed on who had attacked Scott nor how he got to the hospital. But for now, Scott was stable.

"He's in the bed by the window. He's on some powerful drugs right now. I'll be in my office if you have questions," Dr. Falk said then walked off down the corridor.

"Scott?" Ben spoke softly down to the bruised face.

The man in the bed slowly raised a frail fist in the air and gently shook it. His crooked smile showed it was indeed his friend Scott.

"Hey Ben…" his voice was weak.

"Hey, how are you doing?" Ben smiled.

Scott raised his head, looking around. He gestured toward the chair next to the bed and Ben moved it closer, sitting on the edge.

"You feeling okay? That was a big scare. We had no idea…" Ben explained restlessly.

Scott held up an I.V fed hand, "I'm sorry, I didn't…" He struggled for breath. "I don't remember anything…we left the pub…I started walking…"

He fell back to the pillow and fell silent.

Looking up at the large I.V bag, Ben wondered how long before his friend would fall into a long pharmaceutical slumber.

Then, almost a whisper, "I should of known what was gonna happen…"

Scott licked his cracked lips.

Ben leaned closer. "You see who did it? Who took your wallet and watch?"

At this distance, Ben could see the red stains under the gauze on his friend's chest.

Scott sighed, his eyes closed. "No…I didn't see the mugger…or the knife."

A small snore came from his throat and Scott's voice trailed, getting lower in volume with every word, "I saw it Ben….that ambulance…the 50's one…it had its engine running…it was there before the guy got to me…those guys…in white…They were waiting…"

Scott slept.

Ben, however, felt more awake than he ever had. He tried to summon the strength to rise from the chair but his limbs were concrete. The thoughts hardly made sense but there was no denying them.

Leaving the hospital, Ben was careful. He couldn't shake the spooked feeling clinging to his body. His fearful mind raced as he peered in every direction, down every road and side street for any sign of the ambulance. Ben thought of Gregory and the weather vane…the barista… their neighbour Aaron… his friend Scott.

It was lurking, stalking the town, carrying bad luck and accidents like a virus.

It could be coming for him right now.

Parting the net curtains, Lauren placed the Jack-O'-Lantern in the front window.

She couldn't help but feel nervous.

There had been an ambulance parked outside the house for the past five minutes. It was a long white car, almost like a hearse, with white wall tires and a blue rotating bubble light on top with big headlights, each door with a simple red cross on it. It looked like something from the 1950's.

Two men in white sat staring out the windshield towards the house…

…towards her.

THE BONFIRE

Though you may think of November 5th as the day for a bonfire, October is just as an appropriate time as any.

The mourning trees lose their leaves and scatter them down upon the world for all the children and adults alike to kick through with joy and innocence. Some leaves dry blood red, some apple pink or dirt brown, others mustard yellow or pumpkin orange, some even black as coal or blue or purple in some cases. A fall rainbow of colours seen only once a year in nature. During the mild daytime, rakes come out of garden sheds, dusty and cobwebbed. The day is spent clawing the leaves from the grass and paths, collecting them into a heaped pile of treasure in the centre of the garden, not once but twice.

After the first collection, the pile is ripe for taking a run up the garden path and diving feet first into. Swimming in pure autumn with hands reaching out grasping the season, rubbing it between fingers feeling its unique unearthly texture, catching it under the fingernails and getting it lost in the ruffles of hair on your head. Oh to smell the mulch and leaves was better than a hot plate of turkey and gravy on Christmas Day. It's a deep smell, ancient and fresh simultaneously, all the ages of earth and years combined into a single aroma. What better smell to remind you that autumn has arrived. After soaking up and storing the sensation in memory bottles for later, during the icy days of winter and vibrant days of spring, the leaves are gathered together once again upon the dead lawn.

Adults gather as night creeps forward, clutching their warm mulled cider or pumpkin spiced cocktails clad in their winter parkas and cardigans. One of them pulls a small box from a pocket, a box that rattles with a shake of the wrist. Out of the box comes a little red headed solider ready to scrap against the corse siding of the box to come alive with a sizzling pop and a flame of yellow and orange. All the standing people surrounding the high pile of leaves and kindling begin to countdown.

Three…two…one!

And the match is tossed onto the pile which engulfs itself in high fire and balloons of smoke rising up into the darkening orange sky.

A new powerful odour hits the nose and slaps the senses senseless. The burning smells glorious, a smell you can almost taste and it tastes familiar and safe.

It's like being drunk and the liquor was autumn.

Warmth swims around everyone watching, hot on the outside but slowly warming the inner core.

Their reflecting eyes slightly watering, tears of smiles and happiness roll down cheeks. Flickering embers rise above and float like fireflies sweeping across moon.

Fire, fire burning bright, coming forth to light the night.

1928

The table was covered with newspaper and upon the headlines of yesterday sat two pumpkins.

Ray Crane and his grandson Henry sat in the brightly lit kitchen both holding their required tools, Ray with a kitchen knife and Henry with a little plastic saw.

After cutting a circle around the top, they pulled off the lid of the pumpkin, removed the pulpy goodness within, cleaned the smooth flesh of the squash and sat back to consider the vast choice of faces they could carve.

Grandpa Ray leant back, opening the flat tin filled with filtered brown cigars and lit one with a match.

"Any ideas Henry?" he asked, blowing smoke from his nose, down through his white moustache.

"I think..." Henry thought. "A scary face!"

"Well of course scary! It's Halloween!" Ray chuckled.

"What will you do?"

The smoke rose up before Ray eyes as he let it create great mirages on the pumpkin in front of him.

The blue haze curled and twisted and slowly a face emerged.

He smiled, "I think I got one."

"Do you always do pumpkins Grandpa?"

"Oh my yes! It's Halloween tradition! It's something you must do! Ever since I was a boy."

Henry looked in disbelief, jaw nearly on the table.

"There was Halloween when you were a kid? But...but that was so long ago! I don't believe you!"

Ray laughed. The boy's naivety was sweet.

"Halloween has been around for hundreds of

years Henry! Certainly when I was a boy. Well, we may not have had all those pricey costumes or fancy masks you have now but we always had pumpkins, streamers and….well, we managed to celebrate with what we had."

"Wow…so what was Halloween like when you were my age?" Henry asked, forgetting about the pumpkin before him.

"Your age?" Ray pondered. "When I was ten years old it was many years ago, 1928. It was the year Port Hampton cancelled Halloween."

*

Castle Street, the main street in the small village of Port Hampton, had finally been paved and now, Ray Crane and his friends, Sam Fox, Robert 'Bob' Taylor and Harry Frost, could cycle with a lower risk of tire punctures. The town hall had installed a new clock high at the top of the pointed tower for all of the town to see, so now summer days had a time limit.

It was the month of May, the sun was shining and the whole of summer lay ahead of them. School would be finished in less than a month then they could spend lazy days down at The Den, their secret hideaway down by the castle ruins, playing soldiers or reading the comics they picked up at Mr. Raimi's store without the prying eyes of the adults to drag them away to do chores.

However, on a Sunday there was a chore that couldn't be avoided.

Church.

A word that filled Ray with dread and boredom. There was only one church in Port Hampton, it was within the walls of the ruins of the roman era castle and was led by Reverend Hugh Blair, the man who swore by every word printed in the bible. Most of the adults loved him, they saw him as a light in the dark years following the Great War. But to the children, he was the man who yelled a lot about the Devil walking among them and talked of sin and people doing bad things but worse of all, he was the man who made you stay sitting on the hard pews for nearly two hours every sunny Sunday morning of summer.

That Sunday was different though, Ray lay in bed with a nauseous stomach, envious of the sun beaming through his bedroom window. His parents and older brother Michael had left that morning at around 8:30am dressed in their best clothes. Ray got to stay in bed with a bucket next to him, which now, being a optimism, was half full of bile and vomit. His pyjamas were soaked with sweat, sticking him to the coarse sheets. Drifting in and out of sleep for the few hours he was alone Ray tried his best to keep his dry toast breakfast down.

The pebbles on the window brought him back to consciousness.

Peeling himself off the bed, he stumbled to the window and peered down onto the bright street.

Below were Sam, Bob and Harry.

They had already loosened their ties and had grass stains on their knees and their hair ruffled comfortably.

"They voted!" Harry yelled up though cupped hands.

Ray raised the window. "What?"

"Reverend Blair and the adults! They took a vote! He made them all say yes!"

Ray was puzzled for a brief moment then remembered. His eyes widened. "No!"

"They've cancelled Halloween!" The three boys below cried in unison.

*

By noon that day, the boys all congregated down at The Den, now in comfortable dungarees and t-shirts. The Den was simply a small clearing in the woods, enough space for maybe six boys. They had arranged logs to make seats with a small fire pit in the middle. The overhanging low branches made great cover, The Den couldn't be seen from the path and it was easy to duck though the bushes and out of sight from adults and the odd bully alike.

"You should of seen 'em Ray," Bob said shaking his head.

"He was thumping the desk thing, waving his bible. 'An abomination' he called it. Said Halloween was evil and it was something bad to do to God," Sam shrugged tossing away a stray stick.

"They said they ain't gonna be growing any pumpkins this year. None. Old man Weller said he's gonna plant corn instead. Blair got to him back in January and talked him out of pumpkins," Harry explained. "The newspaper guy said they ain't even gonna run the Poe story they usually do!"

"What about costumes? What about the masks and stuff?" Ray asked, no longer feeling the nausea.

"Nope, Mr. Raimi said he's not stocking them. Says he never believed in it anyways. Who doesn't believe in Halloween for God's sake?" Harry asked bemused.

Sam shrugged. "Maybe we can go to Warren Valley? They'll have stuff."

"Yeah and who's gonna take us? My parents were standing up clappin' at every word Blair said. They want nout to do with Halloween," Bob said glumly.

"We can't just not have Halloween! That's insane!" Ray protested. "We can't let it happen!"

"Well what we gonna do Ray? No pumpkins. Unless our parents take us to Warren Valley or even further out to Collingwood but that ain't gonna happen. They're all on Blair's side."

Ray sat brooding over thoughts for a moment, looking for answers in the dirt below him.

The four boys sat quietly.

Halloween was the best day of the year. They couldn't let it slip through their hands. How many years did they have left of it anyway? Though they wanted to deny it maybe Halloween was a thing just for kids, then when you hit a certain age, you put the ghosts and bats in the back of the cupboard like old toys no longer played with but are kept out of some strange feeling of guilt. Ray's older brother, Michael, who was nearly seventeen, had little interest in Jack-O'-Lanterns or spooky masks and bubbling cauldrons. It filled Ray with sadness, to lose one Halloween of the precious few left before growing up, where all the awaited was jobs, bills, girls and misery.

The burst of frantic energy hit him like a lightening bolt.

"Blair can't take Halloween from us! He just can't. Who says he can lead the town? He ain't the mayor!" Ray shook with anger.

"Yeah but Mayor Bennett is behind Blair. He don't want Halloween either," Bob sighed.

"So what can we do about it?" asked Harry.

And, in a way only boys who had been friends for a lifetime can, they each understood what the other was thinking without uttering a word.

Harry picked up a stick and began drawing on the ground, "I think…"

"What about…" Bob started, looking down at the mud doodle.

"And we could…"

"Yeah that'd work…But…Ah I see."

The ideas were clicking into place.

"And you think we can do it?" Harry asked finally and quietly from the log bench.

"I think so," said Ray.

They plotted their plan for the rest of the day.

*

Summer walked over time. The sun rising early in the morning and setting late at night. The warmth still clung in the air allowing for swimming down the creek until late evening and camping in backyards looking up at the stars in the cloudless sky.

It may not have been noticeable but slowly, coming through September, the days got slightly colder, slightly shorter and most certainly, the unstoppable force of autumn was coming.

On the last Sunday of October, the 28th, Blair came to the pulpit, gently placed his bible in front of him then looked out with judging eyes upon his waiting congregation.

"Fall is here." His deep voice boomed in the high ceilinged church. "And Death has come to our town in sweeping form, taking leaves from trees and we must sit watching plants wither and shrivel until they are no more. Our Lord, the Lord Jesus Christ watches over us, protecting us from the evil coming. October 31st, the Devil's day, is nearly upon us. We, the good people of this town, the people who still know the right thing to do, to come to the Lord's house on the Lord's day, decide to rid ourselves and protect our children from such blasphemous ideas as dressing like ghouls and devils. It's unholy!"

He slammed a fist on the pulpit making the whole room jump an inch out the pews.

Blair moved across the platform at the front of the church, his burning eyes never leaving his flock.

"We all opted to discard this wicked day from our lives. Mr. Weller has grown us luscious corn instead of pumpkins, used to create those ghastly Devil faces. Mr. Raimi has refused to stock gruesome costumes and used the shelf space for wholesome Christian literature. Now, we may remember the events during the winter of 1690 and the trials of witchcraft held here in our very parish. Those heretics buried in this very graveyard I'm sorry to say. This Halloween is their day, their abominations of witchcraft and black magic. Their influence, destroying our basic traditional values and causing a negative influence on the fragile minds of our children! We must not have it! Stop the witches orgy and defend the cross! When you wake on the last day of the month, I want you all to know my doors are open to all those who wish to come. I want to remind you of the story of…"

Blair continued, the sweat dripping down from his brow onto his bible and grown ups all agreed with the words spurting from his mouth.

From the pews, Ray, Sam, Bob and Harry tried to stiffen their giggles as they thought of the plan.

Blair wouldn't win.

They wouldn't let him.

*

Tuesday, the 30th of October, came soon enough.

The boys had met during the day to go over the plan one more time, each had their own part they had worked on all summer. They would have little time.

It had taken a long time but they knew they were ready.

They agreed to meet at The Den just after their parents went to sleep, which was usually 10:00pm or 10:30pm, enough time for eight hours sleep, a time figured out after months of timing and observing.

The boys would not be sleeping.

Ray sat restlessly at dinner, looking down at the pork chop with boiled potatoes with an ear of old man Weller's corn. It was his least favourite meal. Excitement was brewing within him, ready to explode from within him like a cold cola bottle fizzing over. Ray reviewed the plan in his head again and again. What if they were caught redhanded? What would happen? Some dire punishment dished out by Blair that would probably last a whole year. He shook the thought from his head.

That was IF they were caught.

Pretending to read a book he had pulled from the living room shelf at random, Ray waited the clock out until bedtime. Then, while in the bedroom full of dark, he listened to his parents climb the stairs and enter their own room.

His bedside clock read 10:26pm. Right on schedule.

Patiently, he waited another half an hour with wide eyes and a pounding heart before he climbed out of bed, dressed and escaped through the bedroom window and out into the night.

Sam, Harry and Bob were already at The Den waiting. They spoke in whispers, confirming details and routes they would take, with flashlights under their chins. All four boys shook with anticipation of doing something mischievous.

The night was chilly but they did not feel it.

"Did you bring them?" Ray asked Bob.

"Yeah, My parents found me makin' some back in September but I managed to hide these," Bob said and pulled out four masks from his bag, handing one to each of his friends.

"Ready?" Ray asked quietly, almost feeling the glee and excitement jumping out his throat.

In the battery powered light, he could see his friends all smile and nod in unison.

They donned their masks.

By dim moonlight shrouded by grey clouds, Ray, Harry, Bob and Sam leaped, ran, jogged, raced, climbed and jumped all across the sleeping village of Port Hampton.

Each boy setting in motion their part of the plan.

Sam threw the black toilet paper he had meticulously used typewriter ink from his father's office to draw a million black bats and cats on. He

tossed them high up into all the trees in the front
yards of Castle Street. Up and down, up and down,
up and down. Giant arcs hanging from every branch.
The beautiful streamers hung like the wrappings of
an ancient mummy from an Egyptian tomb.

Sam wore the ghastly face of a vampire.

Harry had spent the summer going through
neighbour's gardens stealing the odd bedsheet from
unguarded clotheslines. Though they were annoyed,
most of the grown ups simply bought new sheets and
forgot about the missing one. Slowly, over the
months, Harry had accumulated nearly thirty clean
white bedsheets. He drew on silent screams of
phantoms and stuffed their heads with newspaper
giving the spirits their shape. Harry followed quickly
behind Sam, hanging his creations.

His wandering, lost spooky spectres.

Harry wore the mythical grimace of a
gargoyle.

Bob took like a flash down the street, climbing every lamppost then, as he reached the top, he ran a thick paint brush of orange paint down along the already black pole. Halloween candy canes that looked good enough to eat, all dotted up and down the street. They would of been pumpkin and liquorice flavour and Bob couldn't help but smile at how they complemented Sam and Harry's work.

Bob wore the ugly stare of a witch.

Ray flew down the paved street on his bicycle with both his front and back baskets full of papier-mâché Jack-O'-Lanterns. Eight in each basket. All of them the size of the happy birthday balloons from Mr. Raimi's store. All the boys had taken turns in making the pumpkins over the summer, never buying the same orange paint twice in the same week nor another pack of balloons so not to raise Mr. Raimi's eyebrows.

Each 'pumpkin' painted bright orange with black features that looked deep and hollow.

Ray had removed the playing cards from his wheel spokes and now glided silently and carefree. Stopping at one end of the street, he checked the houses for any lights. They had been undetected up until that point but a mistake could expose the whole game.

No lights, they were still undercover and unseen.

Ray snuck up to front porches and front doors and gently placed one of his 'pumpkins' down. The fact it wouldn't be able to hold a candle was unimportant. It was more than just a pumpkin. It was a symbol. Nothing was more identifiable with the beautiful and honoured day of Halloween than a Jack-O'-Lantern, be it an actual pumpkin or, the best the boys could manage, papier-mâché. Up and down the street, Ray crept like a strange All Hallows' Eve Santa Claus dropping off a present for the unsuspecting.

Ray wore the vacant stare of a skull.

At just before midnight, the boys met finally at the lychgate leading into Blair's churchyard. The boys removed their mask and all wore wide grins as they caught their breaths. Their plan had unfolded exactly like they had planned and hoped. The town not only looked, but more importantly, FELT like Halloween. The whole town had the feeling that a ghoul might be lurking in a dark corner or a witch might fly across the moon on her broom.

With the night of the 30th coming to a close, Ray and Sam climbed the sides of the church, scaling each side of the large wooden doors, carrying with them the last of Harry's bedsheets. They tied the corners of the sheet to the aged gargoyles on each side and as the chimes from the town hall clock echoed midnight, they jumped to the ground with a laugh letting the sheet fall and unravel.

On the sheet was painted a giant pumpkin! A wicked face, surrounded by crude skeletons dancing in celebration, smiling down upon the churchyard.

In large green and purple letters: "*Happy Halloween!*"

It was a work of art, not just the bedsheet but the whole town, if the boys did say so themselves.

Blair had lost.

After they returned to their beds, where they lay with open eyes and smiles and full of October spirit, the four friends awaited the rising sun of Halloween morning for their masterpiece to be discovered.

ARE YOU AFRAID OF THE DARK?

"Nyctophobia," Dr. Falk said from behind his desk.

Vincent Jarrod felt stupid. "What does that mean?"

The doctor sighed. "A morbid fear of the dark!"

"Oh, it has a name?"

"Of course! All fears do: triskaidekaphobia, trypanophobia, arachnophobia, Acrophobia. Every fear under the sun has a name. I would say you have severe Nyctophobia," Dr. Falk diagnosed.

Though he could be a cold man at times, Vincent knew Dr. Falk was the most trustworthy doctor in Port Hampton. He always had a firm way with words whereas others simply threw pills at a patient and told them to call in a week or so.

"Well…what can I do about it?" Vincent asked, hoping for the solution.

"I prescribe a lightbulb, Mr. Jarrod," Dr. Falk quipped, looking through his milk bottle spectacles.

After leaving Dr. Falk's office, Vincent went to 'Taylor's' hardware store. Looking up and down the aisle he found the lightbulbs. He had noticed a bulb had burnt out in his kitchen and didn't want to spend another night wondering if more would blow and he'd be left in a dark house.

The idea made his neck sweat and stomach turn.

Through the store's front window, Vincent could see out into the street. The sun was cutting sharp lines across the houses and store fronts opposite. He could almost see the shadows growing as the evening matured. October was the month where this process sped up, sped up much too fast for Vincent's liking.

He stared at the wall of boxed lightbulbs before him and holding out the burnt one from the kitchen, he tried to match it up to the pictures on the boxes.

Eventually a clerk with a name tag reading 'Randy' came and helped.

Vincent needed a E27 screw fit bulb. Randy quickly found one, picked it off the shelf, checked it for cracks then took it over to the counter.

Vincent carried the bulb back to his home like a precious ruby.

The stepladder creaked under his weight, which was not much but maybe enough to make him consider the gym after a heavy meal, as Vincent lifted his new bulb and screwed it carefully into the socket. He reached over fumbling for the light switch as he saw the night start encroaching along his backyard up toward the window of the laundry room.

The lightbulb burst to life with the flick of a switch.

Just in time, he thought stepping down to the floor. He had only been in the new house a few weeks but he had made at least some progress unpacking. Boxes were in the right rooms but still needed going through and sorting. The townhouse had been cheap, especially for Port Hampton, and was still nice with only a little renovation work to be done. A few gaps in the floor boards here and there, a draughty window in the study, a yard that certainly needed a green thumb or two and the bulbs in the kitchen, it was the second time in a week he had replaced them.

*

As he lie under his heavy duvet that night, the bedside lamp on, the autumn winds blew against his window. The attic rattled slightly, just ever so slightly, but enough to just keep him from sleep until his eyelids were too heavy to keep open.

He wondered, as consciousness slipped away, wither he heard his name said in some high corner of the bedroom but was not awake long enough to confirm or deny it.

*

"Nope, I'm afraid I've checked twice now Mr. Jarrod," the electrician said, putting his tools back in his belt. "I can call the electric company and double check but I can't find a problem."

Vincent sighed with frustration, "I've replaced the lightbulbs seven times now."

The electrician shrugged, looking at the fixture on the ceiling. "You thought about changing…"

"I HAVE changed the fixture too. The whole light fixing," Vincent tried to keep his voice calm.

"Well…I…" The pager on the electrician's tool belt beeped. "Ah, looks like an emergency. I can only suggest…well, I don't know."

The man left and all Vincent could feel was despair and panic.

*

Vincent could feel it…It was in the room with him, hiding under the bed. It may not be seen but he knew it was under there. Under the bed it was dark. Not just an absence of light…but darkness itself was breathing and living…waiting…

He wasn't sure, be it a trick of the mind or simply pure anxiety…something was tickling his legs…in the darkness under the quilt, creeping up his leg from his toes. It was cold and almost like, dare he allow himself the thought, a hand. He tossed the quilt from the bed and lay shivering, but completely in light, for the rest of the night.

*

The morning came and Vincent felt safe to turn off the bedside lamp now the sun was bright through the blinds.

He dreaded getting out of bed.

Three different electricians had come to the house and none of them could tell him what was wrong with the house's wiring. Bulbs were now burning out every day, almost as quick as he was replacing them. The bulbs were black and some even seemed to have exploded, leaving a sprinkling of fine glass across the floor. It was affecting his ability to sleep. He found himself walking through the house at odd morning hours looking at each light fitting in the house. It was spreading. At first, it was simply the kitchen, one bulb kept burning out…then two…then all three. Soon it was the living room light burning out, then the hallway, the bathroom…spreading like disease through the house. All would be fine when he climbed into bed but all the bulbs would be burnt out by morning.

It would have to be another trip to 'Taylor's'. Just like the previous day…and the day before…and the day before…and the day before.

*

A week had passed and now the man was back. Every day he'd be in and now Richard was sick of him. The man was scaring customers away who said they'd rather go to Warren Valley for their hardware needs.

"Go check out down the lighting aisle would ya?" Richard asked as he finished filling a can of mixed paint for the waiting customer.

"Why?" Randy asked, arching his neck to look down the aisle just to the right.

A disheveled man was standing with his back to the counter. His hands were shaking, dropping coins onto the concrete floor. From Randy's position he could hear the strange fellow muttering bizarre patterns of words.

Approaching with caution, Randy held his hands in his pockets in an attempt to look casual.

"Can I help…" Randy began.

The man turned with frightened wild eyes and Randy recognised him as Vincent Jarrod.

A five o'clock shadow clung to the Vincent's lower face. His lips were chapped and cracked with dark red dried blood. Unwashed hair and the smell of sweat and urine. He looked like a man who hadn't slept in days, instead spent the hours huffing on a pipe of damaging drugs.

"Oh, Mr. Jarrod. Are you okay?"

"I need lightbulbs!" Vincent screamed loudly enough to startle Randy.

"Okay…what kind?"

Vincent reached into his outside pocket, which was in fact on the inside as his coat was inside out.

Randy took a step back, expecting the worst from the madman before him.

"Jesus…" Randy gasped as, with bloody scabbed hands, Vincent pulled a blackened cracked bulb from his pocket, the dark glass cutting fresh lines in his palms.

"Something is making my house dark! Thirty bulbs! In the last week! I replace them but no no no, something burns them out! Every night! The dark…it wants to kill me! IT WANTS TO KILL ME!" Vincent rambled, waving hands in front of him.

"Okay…" Randy looked to Richard for back up.

"You don't…" Vincent began to shake.

The E27 screw fit bulb was sold out.

"No, I'm afraid you've bought us out. We should get some more next week…" Randy explained, taking a delicate step away from Vincent.

"NO! It's not quick enough!"

Vincent grabbed the front of Randy's coveralls with both hands, crunching the useless bulb into his palms. Randy tried with all his might to pry the feral man off but Vincent's strength knocked them both to the floor.

"I NEED LIGHT!" The fear and madness in Vincent's voice was real.

"Hey hey!" Richard called, jogging toward the alteration as the few remaining customers gawked. He used all his strength to pull Vincent from his friend and the howling that came from Vincent's throat set Richard's teeth on edge, like claws down a chalkboard. The wild man swung a bloody hand across Richard's face, smearing him with blood and slivers of glass from his chin to his eye.

Vincent pulled free, scraping at the floor. "It's trying to kill me!"

He fled the store, leaving the clerks with their injuries and confusion.

"Get the first aid Randy will ya? You alright?" Richard panted, holding his hands clear of his face and seeing their tiny slices and cuts from the broken lightbulb.

"Yeah…Yeah. I'm okay. That's the craziest thing. The guy bought a bulb and left! Now look, comes in every day and gets weirder and crazier!"

*

The night had come.

Vincent Jarrod, tired, weak and manic, crouched huddled in the corner of his bedroom. He had pulled the lamp from his bedside table and now it shone across the back wall of the room. Stark and hard. The old man in the house down the street had yelled and hollered, threatening to call the police. Vincent hadn't meant to kill him but Vincent needed light and the dark was coming. The decision was quick and savage but he was rewarded. He managed to steal a E27 lightbulb to survive the night with.

The bed had been flipped and pressed against the wall and he had thrown all the unpacked boxes downstairs.

No shadows and no dark space.

All he needed was his lightbulb and to stay awake… but…that feeling…that nauseating feeling of dread and regret crept over him.

The dark was near by and Vincent feared, no matter how much he tried, he had missed it and It was festering somewhere.

The fear was confirmed as he watched the lamp, watched the burning bulb slowly dim, the glass growing dark and black, losing its clarity and becoming dull.

The light retreated and the dark pulled itself through the keyhole in the bedroom door, like smoke It entered the room uninvited. The shadows rose up the walls, morphing, contorting, twisting and changing to a ghastly creature of unspeakable horror. It had arms with pointed claws, eyes that formed as holes in the human shaped shadow tore, eyes that laughed and taunted. A body that disappeared into the mass of blackness spreading across the room.

Vincent could not speak nor breath.

The dark before him, through a shredded horrid mouth, spoke in a mocking whisper that scratched in Vincent's ear, like a rusty blade drawing blood.

"Are you afraid of the dark?" It breathed.

The room became completely black as the dark swallowed it, and Vincent, whole.

NECROPOLIS

"I'm getting a cramp Issac!"

"Now now, Glenda dear, I'm sure it's nearly time."

"Hmm…It's getting rather stale in here I must say."

"Well give it a second there…"

"Why? What are you doing Issac?"

"Now just hold on…"

"Will you two pipe down! I'm trying to have a lie in!"

Somewhere in the distance, carried by the chilled wind, came six chimes from the Port Hampton clock. It was a sound everyone in town could hear, be it in their homes, the library, 'The Fox & The

Pheasant'…or even six foot under the town's graveyard.

From the dirt in front of Issac King's headstone (died peacefully, loving husband and father of Miles), a bony finger slowly rose, scrapping away the mud letting the moonlight down into the grave. The first five foot had been hard to get through but best to wait and make sure it was dark and all clear before digging out the final foot.

"Is it time?" Glenda Brown (passed away aged 72. Wife of Charles) asked a few feet of earth away to the left.

"It is dear, see you up top," Issac said.

"Agh! Well I'm awake now, might as well get up with ya," Edgar Falk (his headstone still to be placed) complained.

With a final effort, Issac pushed away the last of his grave and pulled himself to the surface. If he had had fresh youthful lungs, he would of taken a long deep breath but what remained of his lungs were rotted and full of holes.

He shook his bones, feeling the air on the flaps of skin and muscle lining to ribs, femurs and his skull then shivered with delight.

Glenda rose, her perry wrinkle blue dress, though now ragged and discoloured still looked beautiful in the moonlight.

Edgar made a big fuss about pulling himself up, cursing out loud when he left his leg four foot down. He dug back down for it, rummaging shoulder deep.

Issac sat upon his headstone and gazed out across his town. The graveyard was spread across a hill from which all parts of the town could be seen: the castle ruins, the Carnegie library, the quiet houses decorated with all sorts of pumpkins and bunting, Castle Street with it's cafés and shops was slowly switching off, one light at a time as it shut for the night. Why, if Issac strained his grey eyes hard enough, he could even see his old farm on the outskirts of the town. He wondered what Miles and his wife Cathryn might be doing that night.

It had been four long years since he had spoken with Miles. Issac missed his son.

"You know, this bloody critter has been gnawing away all year," Glenda complained.

Sticking her finger into her eye socket, she popped out her one remaining eyeball, letting it swing from side to side until a penny sized beetle scurried out and headed up to the remaining patches of hair she had.

"Quick, get it!" she shrieked.

Issac raised a hand and flicked the bug away before it could hide again.

"Oh thank you, it's been driving me mad. Scratching away back there…and Lord, the cramp in my back," Glenda stretched, her bones popping.

"Hoo-ee!" Edgar hollered, sniffing his armpits. "I ain't too fresh here I'm afraid."

Issac chuckled. "I don't think any of us are. Why do you think they bury us so deep?"

"So how has your first year been Edgar?" Glenda asked.

Edgar sighed, fixing his leg back to his hip. "Lots of thinking time."

"Oh yeah, lots of time for that," Issac mused. "Had many visitors?"

"The wife and kids usually come once a week. First there were tears…now just quiet whispers about day to day life," Edgar groaned with a hint of disappointment.

"Time heals all wounds," Issac said.

"I think I heard them mention your headstone was nearly finished," Glenda looked at the empty space at the head of Edgar's grave.

"Yes, so they say. They've been at it for neatly eight months now. Gotta wait for the ground to settle."

"I'm sure it'll be a fine piece when it's ready," Issac predicted with certainty.

"I'm sure it will, they're good to me," Edgar smiled with an decomposed jaw that hung crooked.

"Isn't it so nice to have visitors, makes you know you aren't forgotten," Glenda said, looking up at the bright moon.

"Well, I know I haven't forgotten anyone alive," Issac said, thinking of his own visitors. Thought he knew few people well in the town, his son came every month, staying usually for an hour with a folding chair (arriving and leaving on the chimes of the clock tower). His son never said more than 'Hello' and 'Goodbye Dad' but Issac knew Miles wanted to talk and that was still comforting.

"I think it needs weeding around here," Glenda tugged at the shrubs growing next to her headstone.

"Hmm…the yard has seen better days hasn't it," Issac looked around him. The chipped headstones, the litter, the fallen angles, overgrown patches of dead grass.

Through the rusted iron gates at the bottom of the hill, the three of them watched a group of young children walk past dressed in the most fantastic and marvellous costumes, all giggles and Halloween spirit.

The sight warmed Glenda's still heart.

"Oh how I've missed the laughter of children. I used to so look forward to them coming to the farm to pick pumpkins. Each year their wide smiles would be infectious."

"Now WE'RE infectious. Decomposing infections," Edgar quipped, though in a whisper so not to draw the children's attention.

The three sat quietly, only the sound of the wind whistling through their old bones.

"What I wouldn't give for a nice Sunday paper and a nice pipe to smoke," Issac broke the silence. He smiled…though he had no lips, they were long gone.

"Ooo or a nice cup of tea with buttered toast for dipping," Glenda added, twirling her grey strand of hair.

"I miss a good radio show, on the sofa on a dark night, rain on the windows," Edgar clutched an invisible glass in his rotted hand. "With three fingers of whiskey on the rocks. Yes, sir, that's my idea of a good night."

The three allowed themselves the sigh of pleasure as they relived their memories.

"I like to think one day...one day we'll have those things back...when we finally turn to dust... one day," Issac hoped, though he didn't quite believe it himself.

"We spend such a long time down there in those coffins, down underneath the dirt," Edgar said quietly, examining the green wound on the back of his hand.

"Yes…so long, and only this one night, tonight, Halloween, are we allowed to breath," Glenda added.

"Yes…one night…" There was audible sadness in Issac's voice.

Edgar kicked a rock at his feet. His shoes were still intact but were filled with oozing flesh and the odd worm wriggling.

"I sure as Hell don't want to spend my only night a year above ground, sitting around my own grave. I've been down there too long. Let's go stretch out legs a bit, take in the night air."

"I agree," Glenda dragged a foot closer then the rest of her body. "I would like to go for a nice evening stroll."

"I don't know…" Issac was conflicted. They could risk exposure to the world outside the graveyard.

"Come on," Edgar pleaded. "Just down to the gate there, maybe along the wall. We'll stay here in the yard."

"Oh please Issac!" Glenda clapped her bony hands.

The sound of trick or treaters floated up the hill.

The three looked down at the gruesome costumes.

Edgar turned to face his undead friends. "Whose gonna notice us when tonight EVERYONE is dressed just like us?"

"We could walk completely unnoticed. Oh what a treat!" Glenda squealed, popping her eyeball back into its socket.

Issac rubbed a finger to the exposed bone of his chin, an old habit from rubbing a long beard when alive.

He couldn't fault the logic of his friends.

"Okay, Glenda dear, Edgar my friend," Issac put his arms around them both. "Let's go live a little."

Together, the three of them stumbled and lurched away from their graves and down the hill toward the world of the living.

THE PECULIAR CASE OF
MR. HAWTHORNE

He arrived with his black case in hand and only the dark suit on his back. He knew no one. The job was a simple one and he was the only applicant. The solidarity suited him and he was fine with the unusual hours. The arrangements he had made over mail with the town's Reverend were set in place ready for his arrival. As he took in his new home and the friendly smiles from locals, he wondered morbidly, how many of them he would meet through his work.

It was in October that the town of Port Hampton found their new mortician.

Reverend Danvers had instructed in his letter to meet at 'The Fox & the Pheasant'.

At 2:15pm, the pub was rather empty. He looked towards the booth where a plump, bald man wearing wire rimmed glasses and a brown cardigan, was bent over a bowl of soup. A white collar around his thick neck.

"Reverend Danvers?" he asked, standing before the table.

The reverend stood. "Ah, Mr. Hawthorne I presume?"

Mr. Hawthorne nodded.

"How are you? Was your journey here okay?" The reverend asked.

They shook hands.

Mr. Hawthorne placed down his case and slid into the booth.

"Well, Mr. Hawthorne, as you know, we are very grateful to have you here. Mr. Craven has been talking of retirement for a few years now but we've struggled to find his replacement. So firstly, thank you for coming."

Mr. Hawthorne smiled.

"Mr. Craven left yesterday so your lodgings are ready for you. There's a bed and furniture so I think you'll be quite comfortable but if there's anything you need, don't hesitate to ask just about anyone in the town. Lots of people willing to help." Danvers sipped his soup between sentences. "You look young though I must say Mr. Hawthorne. May I ask your age?"

"Thirty three."

"Oh how I wish I could be that age again." Danvers chuckled. "To be young…I'm afraid I'm over twice your age, but only just."

The jolliness left the plump man's face.

"You know, I'll be frank Mr. Hawthorne. We average almost twenty deaths a week. Now, of course, most people take their loved ones to Collingwood or Warren Valley as the departed usually pass in the hospitals so you wouldn't have to handle twenty deceased a week, Mr. Craven handled maybe six or seven a week...I'm sure you understand the work."

The two talked for another ten minutes while Danvers finished his soup.

He extended a hand to the mortician again. "I'm sure you'll be a very welcome addition to our community. Though I imagine the children will think of you as a boogeyman of sorts."

*

It stood silent and dark at the end of the street. Its face was dark wood and lace curtains hung in the windows, blocking a view of the inside.

Reverend Danvers unlocked the door and stepped inside.

A bell rang.

To the left of the door, a simple, unassuming brass plaque read a single word: 'MORTUARY'.

After a brief tour of the lodgings and main office, they walked toward the back of the small building which opened up into a modestly sized neatly arranged room of chairs and draped curtain walls.

The chapel of rest.

"And through here…" Danvers lifted a curtain, revealing another door. Fumbling with the keys, he eventually found the one that fit the large lock.

"You know this…" The reverend did not enter the room.

Inside, the harsh light bounced off the gleaming white tiles covering all four walls. The room contained everything required: a large sink, embalming equipment, yellow aprons and gloves hanging from hooks, bottles of every shape and size containing the necessary chemicals, drawers full of thread, needles, waxes and make up, every possible knife, scalpel and surgical instrument. In the middle of the room was a metal examination table with drainage leading to a grate in the floor. On the wall opposite were two metal freezer doors, big enough to walk through. The storage units.

The familiar smell lingered.

Mr. Hawthorne turned and walked back into the chapel, placing a gentle hand on the reverend's shoulder.

"Thank you."

"I must apologise," Danvers shivered. "I've been conducting funerals for nearly forty three years but this room…this room…it still gives me trouble I'm afraid."

"I understand I have an appointment tomorrow," Mr. Hawthorne said, taking a last look around.

"Yes, there's an appointment book on the desk in the office. Mrs. Spencer. Her husband needs…preparing," The reverend patted the perspiration from his forehead and looked concerned. "It takes a certain person to do what you do Mr. Hawthorne."

Mr. Hawthorne smiled as he turned off the light.

*

Mr. Walt Spencer weighed, by Mr. Hawthorne's estimation, twenty one stone and was in his late sixties. The marbling on the skin was clear and although the register book on the main desk said Mr. Spencer had died during his sleep peacefully, his twisted face told a different story. It was pain. He had died alone, face down, on the floor, calling for his wife with his last dying breath. Mrs. Spencer was at her mothers at the time of death.

Decomposition had most certainly begun and it would now be a closed casket funeral. The bacteria had filled his stomach making it look even larger so it sagged almost down to the corpse's knees. It was close to tearing open if Mr. Hawthorne didn't begin work soon. Leaning low, he smelt the usual smell of death. Faeces, urine and rotten eggs might be an appropriate description, it clung in the nostrils. It made some people retch and vomit but not Mr. Hawthorne.

Mr. Spencer's lips and eyelids had been eaten away by the maggots writhing in his body like squatters in an old house, revealing his yellowed teeth (forty years of smoking) and he stared lifelessly in horror at the ceiling. Mr. Hawthorne wondered, as he lay a bare hand upon Mr. Spencer's chest, what the man would say if he could. The chest was soft. Firm pressure with a finger would puncture the skin like wet newspaper, spilling out the man's innards. The mortician wiped his flat palm against Mr. Spencer's torso and lent low, close to the man's head, looking down the length of the bloated, discoloured corpse.

"Mox tuus spiritum corporis voluntatem." Mr. Hawthorne croaked closely to the cold ear of Mr. Spencer and then kissed the dead man's forehead, licking the fluid from his green hued flesh.

*

The next evening, as the gentle rain tapped the windows while the little trick or treaters ran along the street and twilight came early as it did in autumn, Mrs. Spencer sat in the high backed chair in the warm light of the office with her second cigarette in thirty minutes smouldering in her trembling fingers. Her eye make up had run down her cheeks and her hair unbrushed.

A woman in shock. Suggestible and vulnerable.

She and the mortician had exchanged pleasantries and were now sitting in silence, listening to the cutting wind outside.

"Have you…stiffened him?" Mrs. Spencer asked.

Mr. Hawthorne interlocked his long fingers. "Embalmed. Embalming is a difficult process. Your husband was not a suitable…was not suitable for the process. His body has deterioration…"

She cried.

"Now we need to talk about your choice of service. I understand Mr. Spencer has a plot in Green Lawn cemetery near Warren Valley?" Mr. Hawthorne talked over her cries.

She nodded. "Yes. It's a double plot."

"For him and yourself?"

"Yes."

"And you still wish for Reverend Danvers to preside over the service?"

"Yes," she replied simply, pulling a tissue from her sleeve.

"Do you have anything written yourself? Perhaps something you'd like to read at the service?"

Mrs. Spencer frowned and tried to grasp her words. "No…I haven't really thought of…"

"Well, I imagine friends and family would like to hear memories and good times. Can you think of a good time?"

She considered the question just for a moment, almost feeling insulted. "Of course…a time, lots of times we had together."

Mr. Hawthorne leant forward. "Tell me."

"Tell you?" she stubbed out her cigarette and pulled another from her purse.

"Tell me of a good time you had together," Mr. Hawthorne reached over with the large table lighter and lit her third cigarette.

Mrs. Spencer took a long drag on the tobacco. "I remember making him his favourite dinner the night before he…He wanted roasted garlic lamb shanks with buttered mashed potatoes and he had mint sauce and his usual whiskey…"

"That sounds like a fine meal," Mr. Hawthorne complimented.

"Then we…we looked over the photographs from our anniversary. It was only two weeks ago. It was our thirtieth. Pearl. We had wine…and…oh no."

She began to weep again.

Mr. Hawthorne opened the top drawer of his desk and pulled out a small book, wrapped in black leather, and neatly squared it in front of him.

"Would you like to have more good times with your husband?" Mr. Hawthorne spoke softly.

The sound of the coming storm on the windows echoed in the room.

"Pardon?"

"Mrs. Spencer, do you miss your husband?"

"I...yes what sort of question..." she replied stunned, blowing smoke toward Mr. Hawthorne.

"I asked, Do you miss your husband Mrs. Spencer?"

"Yes. I do."

"I would like to make you an offer."

"I don't understand...."

"Would you like to see your husband alive again?"

The question was absurd. Walt Spencer had died and she had learnt at a young age that death was permanent.

"Of course I would. I would do anything…"

"I can make it happen. Nothing is permanent," Mr. Hawthorne said, looking her in the eye.

Had he read her mind? She tried to speak but nothing came out. He was a stern face waiting for an answer. She wanted her Walt back, it was not his time to go. What could the mortician do?

"Would you sign something over to me?" Mr. Hawthorne asked, pulling a fountain pen from his inner pocket.

"Like a contract?" she asked.

"Of sorts yes. I think that is a suitable name for it. You see my little book here? I require your signature on a page."

"Just my name?"

"Not quite I'm afraid. In my field of work, I deal in death. I require customers to continue my work. By signing my book, it simply entitles me to… secure you for my work," he explained slowly and carefully.

"Secure me?" she was puzzled. "You mean you want me to let you plan my funeral?"

"I need to secure you before you pass," Mr. Hawthorne formally said. "To know you fully commit and I can collect your debt once I hold up my end of the offer."

"And…I can see my husband? I sign my name and you'll…you'll bring back my Walt?"

Mr. Hawthorne nodded silently. "He will live for as long as you shall live."

He handed Mrs. Spencer his fountain pen.

A woman in shock. Suggestible and vulnerable.

She took it with a weak hand and held it above the yellowed parchment of the book he slid before her. The cold feeling in her chest welled with a touch of the pen to the page, neither sharp nor dull but there in the centre of her chest. With a shudder she put the gold tip firmly down and began to sign her name. As she curled the E of her first name, a random memory, sensation or feeling crossed her mind, she was reminded of the feeling of stepping out of a warm bath on a cold day but not just reminded…she could feel it under her woollen coat. The feeling of warmth draining down her arm, down into her hand and then left her empty with a sudden feeling of unease and loneliness.

She finished her name looked up at Mr. Hawthorne, who was smiling.

Upon the desk now stood a large antique hourglass. It was a dirty rusted gold colour with cracked glass chambers filled with crimson red sand, all collected in the lower chamber.

"Mrs. Spencer, in one hour, your husband will breath again," Mr. Hawthorne said quietly and as he finished the last word, the sand began to rise, grain by grain, and traveled up through the middle and started to pile at the top of the upper chamber.

Mr. Hawthorne stood and left the room.

Mrs. Spencer sat in silence.

The storm rumbled.

*

The first sound that broke the silence an hour later was her gasp. Her gasp as she saw the grotesque sight of Mr. Hawthorne reentering the room. His apron, though canary yellow underneath was smeared with the dark maroon mix of blood, excrement and bodily fluids. His lower face and jaw were covered with the concoction making him a ghastly figure.

Mrs. Spencer stood, clutching her bag close to her as Mr. Hawthorne stepped toward her.

"What have you done?!" she managed to cry from her tight throat.

"I gave your husband's body life. My half of our deal." he replied simply, the gore dripping from his neatly groomed dark beard. He stood to the side and gestured with bloody hands towards the chapel of rest. "Please."

"He's…he's in there? My Walt?" she began to walk, not taking her shocked eyes off Mr. Hawthorne who stood still as she passed him.

"Walt?" she called into the chapel.

The lights were off but she could sense someone was there.

The sound of drooling, like a dentist sucking saliva from a patient's mouth.

"Walt dear? It's Faye…"

The gurgling continued. Her eyes tried to adapt to the darkness. The open doorway behind her created a defined rectangle of light against the far wall.

The feeling of pressure surrounded her. Claustrophobia seemed not far away.

"Faye?" A faint voice called from the back of the room. It was Walt.

"Are you okay dear? Where are you?" she took another step into the room.

Movement in the side of her eye, the far left corner.

It was the foot she saw first.

As it slid across the carpet, layers of flesh tore and rolled underneath the toes, stripping down to the muscle. It was then the foul smell, the vile stench, hit her, like the odour of a butcher's shop full of raw meat…but rotten, rancid meat. Mr. Spencer moved into the light and Mrs. Spencer couldn't even find the sanity to scream. Her mind shattered as she saw the heinous walking corpse in front of her. Mr. Spencer's jaw hung slack as he tried to talk. She could see his eyeballs, full of distress, moving in their shallow sockets towards her. As he stumbled closer, the blisters covering his legs burst and oozed fluid and maggots down to the carpet. A bone cracked and he fell to his knee and ripping down a fat curtain of skin from his chest exposing the deteriorated muscle and pus yellow layers of fat and greed underneath. The discoloured putrid blood leaked from every hole on his body.

The sounds were as bad as the smell but not as horrific as the sights.

"Help me…" The thing pushed from his rotting throat.

Behind her, Mr. Hawthorne shut the door, sealing her and the thing called her husband in the dark. The last thing she saw in the wedge of light as it receded was her husband's viscera bursting through his fat ruptured gut and falling in a pile between his feet.

It was then she screamed and she screamed loudly.

*

Unlike many years ago, It no longer carried a scythe nor did It wear a flowing black robe covering its weathered bones. It now wore a suit of human skin stretched over its tall frame and walked earth unnoticed and unknown. It knew with coldness, method and precision who was to be taken. It, or the name it had taken, Mr. Hawthorne, knew it had collected two more souls for the Beyond. Mrs. Spencer had died shortly after being reunited with her husband of a massive heart attack attributed to decades of heavy smoking.

Mr. Spencer died, for a second time, with her.

The deal had been completed.

The next day, Mr. Hawthorne prepared both bodies, following the code of practice set forth by the National Association of Funeral Directors & Morticians and stored them in regulation black body bags then ordered for cremation.

*

It was late in the afternoon and Mr. Hawthorne waited, in the slowly coming darkness, until his services were required again.

THE PUMPKIN PATCH

Charles M. Brown stared out over his farm trying to estimate how many babies he had grown that year.

He had been growing pumpkins in Port Hampton since buying the farm from Mr. Weller back in 1947 and this year they were wonderful near perfect pumpkins if he said so himself.

The Brown farm was neatly nestled in the valley, just over a mile from town to the south and was surrounded by woods on the west, north and east sides. It was quiet and that was the way Charles liked it. He was quite content to go up and down the rows of strange fruits, turned each one by hand so his babies wouldn't get flat edges. If you were to look up 'Pumpkin' in a dictionary, there would no doubt be a photograph of a specimen from Farmer Brown's crop.

Each year in autumn, the public would come. Each customer coming to find a pumpkin to slice up for a Jack-O'-Lantern for just one day before throwing it away, forgotten and used up. It felt like losing a prized possession, something he had worked so hard on all year, just to give away for a small handful of coins but there were bills to pay. It was October now and very nearly time to open the gates and let the townspeople in. Charles was conflicted inside, unable to tell if it made him angry to lose a pumpkin or if he enjoyed seeing his babies bring such joy to the children.

Halloween never really appealed to him per say, but it did to his late wife Glenda.

*

It was on the night of October 23rd, while he was listening to *The Witching Hour* program on the radio in the study, that Charles saw the flicker of light sweeping across his crop from the woods. He thought for a flash about stories he had been told as a young man about fireflies but quickly realised it was in fact a flashlight searching in the dark. The light was broken up as it moved, confirming to him it was on the other side of the property fence. He had his suspicions who it may be down there.

He set down his tea cup and feeling rage and fear mingle in his bloodstream, stepped out onto the porch.

"Those damn kids…" he muttered.

There was only the wind.

He could hear no voices nor laughter. Glenda, God rest her soul, had always enjoyed children coming to the farm but it sent shivers down Charles' spine, especially now living alone. Kids had no respect these days nor cared for hard work. They were too much about playing games and causing trouble for the good folks of Port Hampton. Charles had caught some of them last year stealing his pumpkins. Charles had always been told that stealing was wrong but that seemed to be a lesson lost on today's kids who took whatever they pleased. The audacity and selfishness of it all, stealing his hard work. Charles himself had always been a good boy and never caused trouble. He kept his head down and worked hard. Don't ruffle other people's feathers and no one will ruffle yours.

Charles almost lost his train of thought when he remembered the light. He quickly grabbed his jacket from inside the door and started to walk across the farm, shouting out into the dark.

The flashlight waved madly and disappeared into the woods as Charles got closer.

"Stay away from my farm!" he shouted with hands shaking with rage. "You're in big trouble if you come back here! You understand?"

*

Henry Crane came running down the street and only stopped when he was safely outside his own house. Farmer Brown had been onto them. Henry had been stupid to go shining the flashlight around. So close they had been to getting pumpkins. If only Billy Wilkins hadn't dared him, well, double doggy dared him. There was no backing down from a double doggy dare. Henry could of asked Grandpa Ray to just buy him a pumpkin and say he took it from Framer Brown's but Billy would know, Henry wasn't sure how but Billy would know. The pumpkin had to be stolen from Farmer Brown's place and had to be stolen at night. Henry knew he had to do the dare or face the consequences.

*

October 30th.

Farmer Charles M. Brown opened his gates to the public and began to say goodbye to his babies. The people walked up and down the rows, prodding and poking each pumpkin. It hurt him. But bills needed to be paid and he knew of no other way. Maybe he should of considered that offer from the American in town who wanted to buy the whole farm for real estate. Glenda had said no and Charles had agreed...but still, Glenda was dead and she no longer lived on the farm. All he had now were his babies. Selling his babies kept the lights on and helped him get day to day and each pumpkin was important to him.

Charles kept a sharp eye out on the children. None seemed to have come on their own, each with a parent...but who knew what the kids might be thinking.

Henry tried to keep his back turned toward the farmer as he and Grandpa Ray looked for a suitable pumpkin. Looking around for Billy Wilkins or Billy's friend, Tobe Stine Henry saw his neighbour Maya Fox wandering near by. The other boys weren't there.

Henry thought of that morning at school when Billy had cornered him in the playground and changed the dare. Billy now needed to SEE Henry go

onto the farm. Tomorrow night, during their usual
trick or treating session, Billy, Tobe and Henry would
cycle up to the farm and Henry would have to sneak
onto the pumpkin patch, take a pumpkin from right
in front of the house without being caught. Billy had
to actually see Henry do it or Henry would be
'Chicken' for the rest of the school year and no one
wants that name for the whole year.

Henry felt like a criminal returning to the
scene of the crime standing ankle deep in the twisting
vines, though no crime had been committed yet.
There were still many pumpkins down by the house.
He mentally traced a way in and out of the farm that
was quick and easy.

Tomorrow he would have to be very quick.

*

Peddling down the road, leaving behind the
busy town of trick or treating and Halloween glee,
Henry, Billy and Tobe headed toward the dirt road
that snaked through the dense woods surrounding the

Brown farm. Henry could feel his hot breath underneath his skull mask and longed for the cool fresh air of the night. He had already been to the King farm with his sister and dad so he had an alibi of sorts. His dad would assume he was indeed trick or treating and who would notice one less skeleton going door to door on a street full of costumed kids? The three boys would bike back to town before all the candy ran dry and porch lights turned off.

They skidded their bikes to a halt on the dirt, just before the fence.

"Well then Henry, here we are. You ready?" Billy asked beneath his gory zombie mask.

Henry stared out over the pumpkin patch beyond the fence. The stillness was unsettling and while he knew Farmer Brown could barely walk and was nearly a hundred years old or something…there was that sting of fear that Brown's skeletal hand might reach up and…

"Henry?" asked Tobe, pulling up his ugly monster mask.

"Huh? What?" Henry tried to make his voice sound brave.

Billy gave a mischievous smile and pointed to the farmhouse across the patch.

"Now, the dare was to go steal a pumpkin from old Farmer Brown's place…but you know as well as me that Brown is a mean ol' guy who needs a lesson teaching. So I want you…to smash 'em."

"Smash them?!" The prospect shocked Henry.

"Oh boo hoo! Brown loses some pumpkins. It's already Halloween, they ain't gonna last till next year. What's he gonna use them for?" Tobe reasoned.

Henry thought back to earlier that evening carving Jack-O'-Lanterns with Grandpa Ray.

To smash an innocent pumpkin seemed tragic and simply wrong.

"Aww, are ya' chicken?" Billy mocked.

That stupid name again. It made Henry's nose wrinkle like there was a foul smell in the air. No way could he take a whole school year of being called it. June was a long way away. Billy was a popular kid and his commands would spread quickly and every kid on the playground would know Henry's new name.

"How many?" Henry asked, defeated.

Billy and Tobe turned to each other in whispers.

"It's Halloween…so thirteen!" Tobe reported with a smirk.

"So…I smash thirteen pumpkins then that's it? You won't call me chicken at school?" Henry asked as he eyed the one lit window in the farmhouse.

Charles sat bent over the desk sewing together the black fabric. He suspected kids might come to the farm and he wanted to be ready if they did. He had gotten the idea while reading a story by Washington Irving.

Build up the shoulders…a long flowing robe…black boots.

The farmer could barely contain his giggles.

"Yep, that's it," Billy said, stepping aside to let Henry move toward the fence. "Better hurry though, Halloween will be over soon the way you're stalling."

Henry gulped then climbed the fence, dropping down into the pumpkin patch. People say the grass is always greener on the other side but the grass on the farm was dead. The dirt was moist from the afternoon showers and the field was nearly empty with the odd pumpkin seemingly slowly sinking down into the mud.

As Henry crept, low to the ground, his eye still on the lit window ahead of him, the thought did cross his mind, what did Farmer Brown use the left over pumpkins for? Henry's first thought was that canned pumpkin stuff in the supermarket but he wasn't sure if that was even real pumpkin.

Each time Henry passed a pumpkin, he was filled with guilt and each pumpkin seemed more like a gentle sleeper unaware of his intentions. The next one, he told himself as he stepped by them, getting closer to the house. Every pumpkin was a possible member of the doomed thirteen but Henry couldn't stop thinking of his evening with Grandpa Ray and his fondness for Halloween. It was so special to him…and smashing a precious pumpkin would upset Grandpa. 'Chicken' might be horrible but it was not as bad as the thought of Grandpa Ray being disappointed in him.

No. The voice in Henry's mind was loud.

He couldn't do this. Halloween was too special and rare to ruin with such mindless destruction. He stood feeling the wind on his neck, then removing his mask, took a deep breath, feeling the relief. The cool air was cleansing. The moment of peace was much needed but was cut short when he noticed no light in the house, probably Farmer Brown headed to bed after a long day.

Turning on his heels ready to accept defeat, Henry was confronted by the zombie and the monster, with arms stretched out high as they let out screams and howls.

The jolt of fear quickly subsided when Henry heard the giggles of his school 'friends'.

"What's the matter Chicken?" asked Tobe, removing his mask.

"Yeah, you scared huh? Little Henry can't take a dare!" Billy cried crocodile tears.

"I just…I don't want to…Well I can't," Henry tried his best to figure out an excuse, though the truth was probably the best thing to say. He hoped to reason with his friends there in the dark.

WHAM!

Tobe sunk a heavy booted foot into a pumpkin.

Billy laughed and stomped onto the pumpkin next to him…then a double jump into the next pumpkin…and another…and another. The monster and zombie jumped around the field laughing and hooting.

A pumpkin massacre.

The farmhouse remained dark but Henry didn't want to be near when Farmer Brown awoke and saw the carnage.

He turned to leave, run away back to trick or treating, to be a good boy and do Halloween right. But the sharp breeze cut through him and he heard the volume of its howl drop and fall to a silence, only the sounds of Billy and Tobe's mean laughter could be heard.

The woods, the bicycles and escape suddenly seemed very far away.

The strange sound made him look back over his shoulder.

Standing in a rotten black cape, a cape that moved like cloth through water, a towering figure stood menacingly. Its body a mass of twisted and snarled vines, mud muscles and root bones all rising to form the shape of a man.

No head.

Its right branch like hand held up a burning Jack-O'-Lantern. A face of rage and punishment.

Henry had heard his Grandpa Ray talk of the very spirit of All Hallows' Eve walking the land on the final night of October and now Henry was certain he was in its presence.

Billy and Tobe seemed oblivious as they continued their 'fun', destroying the pumpkin patch.

The headless monstrosity slipped a primal and bloodcurdling groan from its flaming pumpkin head and pointed a long finger towards the woods.

Henry never stopped running.

Charles M. Brown chuckled to himself as he tiptoed down the hallway.

His costume was perfect, it looked just like the ghostly headless horseman of Sleepy Hollow.

He'd come rushing out, scream as loud as his voice would possibly allow and chase those damn kids away once and for all. He had to keep his pumpkins safe.

His excitement was hard to contain but he paused as he passed the large stain glass window that gave a view across the farm.

Opening his costume and pressing his nose against the cold glass, Charles could see a solitary figure running across his farm to the woods.

The lone figure was running from a small fire burning angrily.

And…perhaps it was the trick of the moonlight or the distortion of the coloured window glass or even the early raindrops of the imminent storm on the glass panes, but the fire was pulling what looked like…people.

Two people being dragged down into the mud.

The flame sunk deep into the pumpkin patch and all disappeared and there were the screams of children on the wind.

Something had protected his babies.

NOVEMBER

Though the seam was invisible, the line between October 31st and November 1st was there. It came just as the town hall clock tower chimed twelve midnight. It was safe to extinguish the Jack-O'-Lanterns on the front porch, the spirits returned to their graves for another year, bats flew away to their dark caves, the chill disappeared, the dense feeling in the air let up and let you breath. The wind sounded different, perhaps it was a different key blowing through the empty trees. The smells were different, they were no longer mysterious. The darkness was suddenly void of its threat and mystery. Halloween, and all of its traditions and splendour, slumbered deep in the pumpkin patch, in under stair cupboards and spider filled attics for another whole year.

The storm, violent and unforgiving, swept through the town and wiped it clear of October's soul and Halloween spirit and cheer.

In the closing months of the year 1990, October became a distant memory and December with promises of a Merry Christmas and a happy new year became the talk of the town named Port Hampton.

This book was started in

Portsmouth, England - September 2017

and finished in

Salem, Massachusetts, U.S.A - February 2018

- J.J

ACKNOWLEDGEMENTS

Lots of people helped me write this book. People I can't thank enough for being there when I would send across a story at 2am wanting notes and those people who provided those notes.

<u>Very Special Thanks to:</u>

Lauren, for the enthusiasm.

Mandy & Anya, for my favourite possession, the 'Olivetti Lettera 22'.

Lara, who read close to every draft of every story and always loved them. My dear October friend.

Scott, my partner in crime, who I began storytelling with so many years ago and who always keeps my ambition lit to tell more stories.

Sam, thank you for chasing scarecrows with me.

Camille, I'm sorry about the constant clanking of the typewriter but thank you for your patience and support.

My brother and sister I want to thank, for many

Halloweens growing up making bin liner costumes and trick or treating for yogurts, coins or whatever else the unsuspecting and unprepared neighbours of Portchester had to offer.

My mother for love and letting me try (and fail) to grow pumpkins in the garden every year.

My father for loaning me the money to rent *The Halloween Tree* on VHS from 'Prime Time Video', sparking my lifelong love in the holiday.

The writers, filmmakers and storytellers who adorn my wall, bookshelves and film collection. I cannot thank them enough and hope I can thank them in person, someday, somewhere in someway:

Ray Bradbury

(For 'The Halloween Tree' & Green Town, Illinois, U.S.A)

John Carpenter

(For 'Halloween' & 'The Fog')

Raymond Chandler

(For Philip Marlowe & Glimpses of 1940's Los Angeles)

Wes Craven

(For 'The Last House on the Left' & 'The Hills Have Eyes')

Michael Dougherty

(For Sam & 'Trick 'r Treat')

Bob Dylan

(For 'Like A Rolling Stone' & 'Chronicles: Volume One')

Alfred Hitchcock

(For 'Psycho' & 'Rear Window')

Tobe Hooper

(For Leatherface & 'The Texas Chainsaw Massacre')

John Katzenbach

(For Francis Xavier Petrel & 'The Madman's Tale')

Stephen King

(For 'Christine' & 'Secret Window, Secret Garden')

H.P. Lovecraft

(For Cthulhu)

Sam Raimi

(For 'The Evil Dead' Trilogy)

George A. Romero

(For 'Creepshow' & 'Dawn of the Dead')

Charles M. Schulz

(For Charlie Brown & Snoopy)

R.L. Stine

(For 'Goosebumps' & 'The Nightmare Hour')

Dr. Hunter S. Thompson

(For Gonzo Journalism & 'The Rum Diary')

Thank you all.

The author in Salem, MA, U.S.A

ABOUT THE AUTHOR

Juno Jakob was born in Portsmouth, England in 1990.
He graduated from The Arts University College at
Bournemouth in 2012.

'The October Season' is his first collection of short stories.

He celebrates Halloween every year.

Twitter: @junojakob

Printed in Great Britain
by Amazon

86706572R00140